LOVE ME LIKE YOU DO

Winter Lake

RHIAN CAHILL

Rhian Cahill

Love Me Like You Do
Winter Lake
By Rhian Cahill

For more information visit:
www.rhiancahill.com

Love Me Like You Do
Love The Way You Are
When You Love Someone
Let Me Love You
Wild Rush Of Love

LOVE ME LIKE YOU DO
WINTER LAKE BOOK 1

First comes love, then comes marriage, then comes baby…
wait, scratch that. Can we start with the babies?

Selling most of her possessions, breaking her lease and driving across the country in search of a man who might not want to see her probably wasn't such a great idea. Throw in an aging car with no heat, snow covered mountains and a rapidly expanding pregnant belly and Covington Valenti may have made the biggest mistake of her life.

When the woman who's had him twisted up for over a year turns up in Winter Lake Tristan Harding is more than happy to see her. What he's not so sure about is her extra baggage. But Tris is nothing if not a loyal friend and if Cov needs his help she has it—even if that means stepping up for someone else's kid.

For those, like me, who love small towns

CHAPTER 1

The car stuttered...

"*No, no, no, no.*"

...gasped and choked and bucked...

"*No, no, no, no.*"

...and kept going.

Rubbing her hand on the dash, Covington crooned, "That's it, baby," and prayed her beat-up Cavalier Z24 would make the last few miles.

"Just a little more. It's not far now and I promise when we get there you can stop, fall apart, die. Whatever you want. Just give me a little more. *Please*," she begged as she continued to stroke the cracked dash.

When the car continued up the road, she let out a slow breath and tried to focus on the positives.

The car was still moving and she was getting closer to her destination with each mile.

Except it was hard to keep an upbeat attitude when

nothing had turned out the way it was supposed to—the way she'd planned.

For one thing, she was freezing. The aged heating system and flimsy roof of her convertible couldn't compete with the cold seeping through every nook and cranny.

There was also the fact she was thousands of miles from home looking for a man who more than likely didn't want to see her.

Oh! And the kicker. She was four months pregnant.

With twins.

Sniffling, she turned the heater knob another notch and hoped the change didn't cause the car to quit.

The engine didn't die but the air blasting through the vents didn't get any warmer either.

"He probably hates me," she muttered, the white cloud forming in front of her face growing bigger with every word.

She hadn't seen Tristan Harding since the morning she'd kicked him out of her bed.

Four months ago.

By the time she'd gotten over the fact she'd slept with him. Over the fact he wasn't the man who'd put a ring on her finger. Over the fact she'd felt far more for Tris than she ever had for Gavin. Over her own stupid embarrassment and shame...

Tris was gone.

She didn't dare ask anyone where he'd disappeared to though.

Especially not Gavin.

After catching her fiancé screwing one of her fellow

dancers, Covington hadn't said anything to the lying, cheating scumbag.

Nope. She'd taken off his ring, left it on his dining room table—along with the key he'd given her to his apartment —and driven home.

Where she'd promptly set about ridding her place of every little piece of Gavin and the plans he'd shattered by dumping all his stuff out her third floor window.

That's when Tris had showed up.

She'd been leaning out the window with a bundle of Gavin's clothes in her arms ready to let them drop when he climbed out of his truck.

Tris had looked up at her, looked down at the growing pile of crap on the lawn, then brought his gaze back to hers and smiled.

She had to admit he'd made her tummy flutter more than once in the year and a half they'd known each other, but *that* smile, the way his eyes creased at the corners, scruff covering his chiseled jaw and his dark hair ruffled by a light breeze...

Damn, she'd fluttered in places lower than her belly.

Covington couldn't say why she had done it. Why she'd let him in, let him help her purge her life of the scumbag, or why, after a shared pizza, a couple of beers, and some great conversation, she'd let him into her bed—into her body.

That was a lie. She knew exactly why.

The man had moves. His lips and hands had her pulsing with arousal with the barest touch. And he'd touched her.

Everywhere.

Not that he'd been the only one. Oh no. She'd gotten her fair share of groping in before they'd stripped naked and engaged in the best, most mind-blowing sixty-nine she'd ever been part of.

Her sex clenched with the X-rated memories flashing through her head, a tremor quaking her from head to toe as her core temperature rose without the help of the car's ancient heating system.

He'd done things—*she'd* done things—that put every other sexual encounter she'd ever had in the amateur's league. She couldn't explain why she'd allowed Tris to touch her in ways she'd never trusted any other man to do. And that included her cheating, lying scumbag ex-fiancé.

"Goddammit!" She slapped the steering wheel with a gloved hand.

The car jerked and shuddered, lurched and bucked.

"Please don't die," she whispered as she firmly wrapped her fingers around the wheel again and hoped she didn't hit a patch of ice. She'd heard that could be treacherous.

Born and bred in Los Angeles, she hadn't been prepared for the cold. Or the snow. There was no escaping it. It was everywhere.

When she'd stopped in Saratoga Springs for gas and munchies, and gloves for her freezing fingers, the old guy behind the counter had chatted away about the lack of 'inches' on the ground for this time of year and the unseasonably warm temperatures.

But if her frozen body and what she'd seen on the drive through the mountains were any indication, there was already way too much of the white stuff covering the ground as far as she was concerned, and Covington wanted to turn right back around and head for places warmer—head home.

Her bottom lip quivered.

"I don't have a home."

She sniffed back the sting of tears, blinking furiously to ward off another crying jag.

"Damn stupid hormones."

She'd given up her lease. Sold everything she could, donated what she couldn't, and piled the few possessions she'd decided to keep into her twenty-two-year-old car and headed for New York.

The state.

Another world away.

Up a godforsaken mountain covered in snow!

When that little blue plus sign had appeared in the teeny tiny window on the plastic stick, Covington hadn't been able to breathe. It had taken her a very long, very angst ridden day to come to terms with the fact she was pregnant.

After the initial shock wore off, she'd been okay with the idea. More than okay. She'd been thrilled to know she was carrying Tristan's baby.

But then morning sickness set in and dancing had become difficult. She lost her balance as well as her lunch and a couple of one-day jobs along with them, and as she headed into the third month, and her weight dipped to an all-time low, she panicked more than a little.

Surely it couldn't be normal to lose weight while growing another human being?

Her doctor had assured her she was fine—the *baby* was fine—but scheduled an ultrasound 'just to be on the safe side' and put her mind at ease.

There was no 'safe side' for what that scan revealed and no easing of the mind.

Hard to ease the mind when it had been blow apart by two miniature hearts beating fast and furious as two perfect little bodies formed and grew.

"*Oh god.*" Her fingers clenched on the wheel as her stomach clenched around two bags of chips, three cans of soda, and one and half bags of gummy bears.

The rush of fear and excitement and panic shot through her as quickly and sharply as it had two weeks ago when she'd first seen with her own eyes the teeny lives she and Tris had made.

She'd stumbled out of her doctor's office, vaguely remembered thanking him and paying the bill, and somehow found her way home while her world spun and tilted all over again.

She couldn't do it alone.

One baby would have been manageable and she'd had every intention of hunting Tris down to let him know he was going to be a father, but *two* babies...

Covington might pride herself on her independence and know she could, if push came to shove, do anything she set her mind to. But raising two babies while working in an industry that required she stay in peak physical form when in all likelihood she'd be forced to rest later in her pregnancy not to mention most singers didn't want a pregnant woman in their music video, then there would be night feeds once the babies arrived...

Well, there really was no way she could do it alone.

She sighed.

She'd been deluding herself.

She didn't *want* to do it alone.

Hadn't from the moment she'd discovered she was pregnant. And when the situation had sunk in and the reality of having Tris's babies had taken root in her mind as firmly as they had in her belly, well, she could no longer deny her true feelings.

Finding him had become a priority.

Ironic that it was Gavin who'd revealed Tristan's whereabouts.

Her ex-fiancé had turned up on her doorstep accusing her of sabotaging his friendship with Tris and blaming her for Tristan's decision to relocate to that 'godforsaken mountain' miles away.

It had taken a while to get the details out of a clearly drunk Gavin, and even longer to fend off his sloppy advances, but once he'd clued in to the not so obvious swell of her belly—she'd had to spell it out for him—he'd escaped her apartment building as though his ass was on fire.

A little more investigation and Covington had all the information she needed on Tristan's new home and made the decision to pack up and move there too.

She had to admit she was excited to be going to Tristan's hometown. He'd told her so much about the mountains and the lake where he'd grown up that she felt as though she'd been there already. And it sounded like the perfect place to raise children.

Surely there was a dance studio she could get work at or maybe start her own. Now that she was pregnant, the idea of teaching little kids to dance appealed. It never had before but now...well the thought alone gave her a thrill. She could work around the demands of pregnancy and when the babies came and needed her attention.

The plan made sense, even if it was a little vague and didn't take into account Tristan's reaction to seeing her.

"Lord, what if he won't even talk to me?"

The car drifted as she rounded a bend on the slippery mountain road and her fingers flexed, her hands tightening on the wheel as she eased off the gas.

Driving in snow country definitely required full concentration. The last thing she needed was to end up in a wreck. At this point, the Cavalier was her only means of shelter and crashing it would put her in an even worse position.

"I am such an idiot." She wanted to thunk her head on the steering wheel.

She'd given up her home and most of her belongings and driven thousands of miles with no place to land. Not exactly the best decision she'd ever made. She should have called. Except telling Tris he was going to be a father over the phone felt wrong and she'd already denied him the first few months.

Not that that was her fault; it wasn't like he'd even told her he was leaving.

Okay, sure, she'd kicked him out of bed then out the

door, and she couldn't remember exactly what she'd said to him but Covington had no doubt it wasn't good because the man hadn't just left her apartment, *he'd left town!*

Hell, he'd gone to the other side of the country to get away from her.

With another deep sigh, she accepted the fact the next few hours would be some of the most difficult of her life.

She had to tell the man who'd fathered her children he was going to be a dad. Convince him she hadn't kept him in the dark on purpose, and hope he let her stay with him until she worked out some other arrangement.

Up ahead a sign at the side of the road made her lips twitch with a smile, made her a teeny tiny bit optimistic. As it flashed past, her smile bloomed.

Just the name Winter Lake made her heart swell, made her think of Tris and his obvious love for his hometown. He'd always spoken of the mountain town with such fondness whenever he shared a childhood memory.

No, she would not doubt her decision anymore; the warmth filling her proved she'd made the right choice.

Everything would be okay.

She couldn't—*wouldn't*—entertain any other option.

CHAPTER 2

TRIS FLOPPED onto his bunk at the station house, his body limp with fatigue, every muscle screaming with pain after his session in the gym where the head trainer had done exactly as Tristan had asked and delivered a punishing workout. But it didn't help; nothing Chuck put him through helped. His mind remained alert and spinning around the one subject he'd tried every day for the last few months to erase.

Covington Valenti.

No matter how hard he worked or worked out or drank, he couldn't remove the images of Cov naked and writhing beneath him from his head.

One night and she'd marked him for life.

He'd known he was hooked on the woman the second his former friend had introduced them, but with Gavin's ring on her finger there was no way Tris could make a move.

For over a year he'd watched the man he'd once called friend demolish any respect and loyalty Tris had for him.

Keeping his mouth shut about Gavin's cheating had been torture. Tris had struggled with the dilemma every day until he'd finally had enough and gone to Cov's place with the intention of telling her everything.

Except she'd already known.

God, he wished he could have spared her that heart-breaking discovery.

Although he had to admit he hadn't seen one tear. Anger, frustration, embarrassment, they were all there, but not for one second did she appear heartbroken by Gavin's behavior.

It was why he'd made a move.

And fucked everything up.

He'd never forget the look of pure bliss on her face when she'd come apart in his arms. Never forget the sheer joy of joining his body with hers and pushing her over the crest once more, this time going right along with her.

Nor would he forget the slumberous grey eyes, smoky with satisfaction, that blinked awake the next morning.

Or the rush of dismay and horror that stole away her contentment as she'd registered who was in bed with her.

His plan had been to let her wake slowly before loving her all over again.

Except Cov had other ideas, and all of them were filled with shock and shame and embarrassment.

He'd tried to argue. Tried to get her to see reason except by the time she'd pushed and shoved and maneu-vered him to her front door, his clothes a bundle in his arms, she'd been in tears and Tris had known there was no way to get through to her in that moment.

Yanking on his pants, he figured he'd give her some time to settle then they'd talk, except her parting words had sliced through him as though she'd thrust a dagger into his chest.

"Tell that lying, cheating, worthless scumbag I fucked you for revenge. Tell him how I swallowed. That'll give him a kick in the nuts knowing you got what he never did."

Her laughter had followed him into the hall as he'd flung open the door and left.

"Jesus." Clenching his abs, he curled off the bed into a series of sit-ups in an attempt to banish the latest round of memories.

The bunk wasn't the best surface to work on. It gave beneath him, squeaked in protest as he ramped up the speed and drove himself deeper into the pain and sweat of pushing his body beyond its limit.

"Harding!" A hand slapped down on his shoulder, stopping him from rolling up again. "Shit, man, give yourself a break before *you* break."

Tris blinked sweat from his eyes and the grim face of Devlin Wallis came into focus.

His friend and workmate shook his head. "I don't know what the hell is up your ass but you need to get a handle on it. Yank it out. You'll kill yourself at this rate."

Shoving his friend's arm away, he swung his legs over the side of the bunk and sat up. "I'm good. Just cooling down."

Dev laughed. "Yeah, tell that to someone who doesn't

know what a hard workout looks like or that Chuck just whipped your ass at the gym."

Tris watched as his childhood buddy sat on the bed across from him. He could tell Dev was winding up to say something and really didn't want to be on the receiving end of whatever it was, but he owed Dev.

Owed his friend for getting him in the door of Winter Lake's only fire station and in front of Chief Murdock when Tris had made the decision to move into the house his Great Aunt Josie left him. So he waited.

"Look." Dev ran a hand down the back of his head and gripped his neck. "I know something chased you up here and I've let you stew, hit the bar with you in those first few days, tagged along on more workouts than I need in my lifetime, never mind a few months, but it has to stop. Whatever you're running from is eating you alive, and you need to deal with it some other way."

Tristan's lips twitched. "You get a psychology degree when I wasn't looking?" he asked.

"No. But I know you. And at the risk of taking a fist to the face, I'm going to go out on a limb and say it's a woman who has you all in knots."

He glanced away. Couldn't look his friend in the eyes and lie to his face. "Nah, just had enough of the hot weather, the crazy traffic. Needed to feel some snow under my board."

"Bullshit." Tristan's gaze snapped back to Dev who held up a hand. "I don't want any details so you can keep your lies. Just stop killing yourself. It's killing *me* watching you."

Tris could see the genuine concern in his friend's eyes

and vowed to pull his head out of his ass. But he couldn't do that without closure and this thing between him and Covington would remain wide open until he dealt with it —with her.

They needed to talk.

He couldn't avoid it any longer. The minute his shift ended tomorrow morning he would call Cov and see how she was doing. He knew through his limited conversations with Gavin that the two of them hadn't gotten back together, but that didn't mean she hadn't moved on with someone else.

Even if she was still single, *he'd* moved on—started a new life. He might still be crazy about the woman and if she turned up on his doorstep he'd definitely invite her in, but that didn't mean he'd change his mind about relocating to Winter Lake.

The small town in the Adirondack Mountains had been an oasis in the middle of his chaotic childhood and the minute he'd driven into town three months ago, he'd known he'd made the right decision—this was where he was meant to be.

"Come on. The chief wants us to dig up that area out front. His wife wants to put in some sort of garden, something about bulbs and spring and brightening up everything. Hell, I don't know, all I know is whatever Mrs. Murdock wants, Chief Murdock makes sure she gets."

Tris groaned at the idea of shoveling dirt. He wasn't much of a gardener but he didn't think it was the right time to be putting in a garden. The ground had already started to freeze as winter approached. It would be back-breaking work digging up that area.

Dev got to his feet and grinned. "That'll teach you for pushing yourself too hard."

"He saw me come in, didn't he?" Tristan's thigh muscles protested as he stood.

"Yep." Dev thumped him on the back. "Who do you think sent me in here?"

Great. The last thing he needed was for Chief Murdock to think his head wasn't in the right space or he couldn't pull his weight.

He had two more weeks of probation, then he'd be on the payroll permanently. Tris didn't want to screw this up.

He'd fucked up enough in the last few months so in spite of his aching body, he hauled ass outside and started digging up the hard-packed earth beside the stationhouse driveway.

They were halfway along the roped-off section—him, not Dev, doing most of the heavy lifting—when the chief came out and stood behind them. Murdock didn't speak and Tris wasn't about to open his mouth and invite conversation.

He shoveled and tossed. Shoveled and tossed.

The hiss and grind of an engine in bad need of servicing echoed up the street, breaking his rhythm for a moment. Tris shook his head and kept shoveling.

Someone was in for a world of hurt if they didn't get that thing to a mechanic soon.

"What the hell is that?" Dev asked as he straightened and leaned on his shovel. "Jesus. It looks like a Cavalier."

A Cavalier? Tristan's head swung towards the road as he stood upright. He blinked several times but the snot-green vehicle continued to limp its way up the street.

Turning, he took a step forward. "Cov?" The closer the car got, the more certain he became.

Dropping his shovel, he jogged to the curb as the car jerked to a stop with an ear-splitting screech in front of the station, steam billowing from beneath the hood as the engine coughed and died.

Jesus.

She'd driven the thing all the way from LA.

He raced around to the driver's door and yanked it open.

"H-hi." She smiled up at him sheepishly.

"You drove this piece of shit all the way across the country? What the hell were you thinking, woman?"

They weren't the first words he thought he'd say after months apart, but right now all he could think about was Cov stranded on the side of the road somewhere in the middle of nowhere.

"Um..."

"What are you doing here?"

"Well, um." She glanced behind him and he realized they had an audience. "Can we talk somewhere private? Somewhere warm maybe?" she asked, her voice soft and wobbly.

Crap.

She was bundled up like an Eskimo in what looked to be three hoodies, a couple of different colored scarves, and fluoro yellow gloves, and it wasn't even cold enough for him to put on a jacket over his department issued t-shirt.

Even with all those layers, her cheeks and nose were bright pink and she was shivering.

"Yeah. C'mon, let's get you inside." He offered her a hand and she placed a gloved—tag still on—one in his.

"I can't believe how cold it is up here," Cov mumbled, her teeth clicking together, as she swung her legs out of the car to stand. She'd barely lifted her ass off the seat when she sucked in a breath and dropped back down. "Oh. Oh. Oh. Oh."

"What's wrong?" he asked, as she snatched her hand back and wrapped her arms around her waist, hunching forward.

"I have to pee." She looked up at him with panicked eyes. "Now. I have to pee *now*."

"You can use the bathroom inside," Tris offered, confused by her obvious distress.

"Where? How far?" Her gaze darted to the station entrance.

"Right inside the front door and down the hall." Tris gripped her elbows and pulled her out of her seat and against his chest. Except she didn't press into him like she should have. He didn't have time to contemplate the situation before she pulled away.

"I gotta go." On her feet now, she crossed her legs and bent at the middle. "Where? Where's the bathroom?"

"Inside, to the left—"

"Move." Cov pushed him aside and dashed around the open car door before racing in an ungainly fashion for the front door of the station house. He'd never seen her move so awkwardly. She was a dancer. Every move she made was fluid, graceful.

"What the hell?" Dev muttered behind him.

Tris glanced over his shoulder at Dev then Chief Murdock, and shrugged. "I have no idea."

Murdock laughed. "Nothing more dangerous than a pregnant woman who has to pee."

"*W-what?*" Tris choked out.

The chief tipped his chin in the direction Cov had taken. "Pregnant women. It's life-threatening to get in their way when they have to go."

Tristan opened his mouth to speak but nothing came out. His gaze shot to the door Cov had disappeared through.

Pregnant

CHAPTER 3

COVINGTON BURST into the women's bathroom and stumbled toward a stall. She couldn't get the door closed and her pants down fast enough, and with the desperate need to pee her sole focus, she tripped sideways and bashed into the wall before she managed to spin around and lower herself—pants down—to the toilet.

A breath of relief rushed from her lungs, the knot of tension in her stomach starting to loosen as the knowledge of making it sank in.

She flinched, her sigh of relief turning to a hiss of shock as her backside hit the cold seat.

Muscles clenched, her whole body recoiling from the icy slap to her ass and thighs. It took a moment for everything to unclench and the floodgates to open. And as the pressure drained out of her, she wanted to get down on her knees and thank the pregnancy gods that she'd made it to the bathroom without embarrassing herself in front of Tris and two strangers.

Unfortunately that particular humiliation wasn't new to her; she just preferred not to live through it over and over again.

Of course with the pressure off and the urgency gone, she had nothing to concentrate on except the reason she was here.

Telling Tristan he was going to be a daddy.

She wanted to hide out in this surprisingly well-appointed bathroom and avoid the conversation that was probably pointless now.

She'd heard one of the men outside with Tris when she'd made her less than dignified dash for the bathroom say something about pregnant women and their need to pee, but she'd had other things to worry about and didn't feel too guilty for having her 'condition' revealed in such an in-your-face manner by someone other than herself.

And she hadn't missed the brief look of confusion that crossed Tris's face when he'd pulled her into him and her belly had bumped his. She might only be four months but with two babies on board she'd already 'popped', and with how lean she was everywhere else because of every day, all day morning—*ha!*—sickness, it was obvious to anyone with eyes that she was pregnant.

"How you doing in there?"

Covington jerked, made some sort of strangled animal sound, and almost toppled off the toilet.

One hand splayed on the door in front of her, the other wrapped around the toilet roll holder in a death grip to stop herself from pitching face first on the floor with her pants around her knees, she sucked in a breath and mumbled, "Ah. Okay?"

"Tris wanted me to check. You've been in here a while. Do you need anything?"

He'd sent someone to check on her? "Um…no." As an afterthought she added, "But thank you."

Figuring she was out of time, she did what she had to and flushed. Tugging up her sweatpants, Covington wiggled and rocked her hips in an attempt to inch the waistband over her rounded belly.

The elastic was growing tighter with each day and she conceded her limited wardrobe would become nonexistent in the coming weeks. She'd have to rectify that sooner than later.

Sighing, she gave up and left her pants rolled low on her hips knowing the layers of sweaters would hide her wardrobe malfunction and took a fortifying breath.

She opened the stall door and moved to the sink to wash her hands, trying to ignore the woman leaning against the wall watching her with a speculative gaze.

Washing her hands for longer than necessary, she hoped the woman would leave but when Covington finally turned the tap off she remained, posture relaxed, gaze sharp.

"You're from LA?" It was posed as a question but Covington was pretty sure the woman just wanted to confirm something she already knew.

Nodding, she ripped off a piece of paper towel. "Yep."

"Long way from home."

"Hmm…" Covington hummed in reply.

"Staying?" the woman persisted.

Covington shrugged.

Putting her hands up with a chuckle, she pushed off the wall with her shoulders and said, "All right. All right. I get it. None of my business."

Smiling, Covington dropped the wet towel in the trashcan and moved toward the door. "I should..."

"Yes, you should. Harding is wearing a trench in the tiles waiting outside."

"What?"

"Never mind. I'm Dana, by the way." She opened the door and held it, motioning for Covington to pass through first. "After you."

"Thanks. I'm Covington."

"Unusual name."

"My mother's hometown and definitely better than the other option." At Dana's arched eyebrow Covington added, "Mallow—one town over in case you're curious—was behind door number two."

"Perhaps a third door...?"

"Considering they were getting worse?" She laughed, shaking her head. "I think I ended up with the best outcome."

Dana smiled and indicated the open door. "Shall we?"

Taking a deep breath, Covington raised her chin and steeled her resolve.

She could do this.

She would do this.

She *had* to do this.

Tristan deserved to know and she needed someone to share the load with. Share the joy.

Her heart skipped at the thought of getting to hold their babies. Would they have boys or girls? One of each? Would they look like her or Tris?

"There you are." Tristan rushed at her as she stepped into the hall, his grip on her shoulders stopping her in her tracks, his worried gaze scanning her face. "Are you okay?"

"Yes." She frowned. "Why wouldn't I be?"

His eyes lowered to her belly.

"Oh, right. Um..."

"Come on." He let go of her shoulders and offered a hand. "The chief said we could use his office to talk."

Nodding, she took his hand and let him lead her down the hall, deeper into the fire station.

"I can't believe you drove all the way from LA in that junker of yours. How long did it take you to get here?" Tris asked, as he ushered her into a meticulously neat office and closed the door behind them.

"Um..." She'd left early Monday morning and today was Wednesday afternoon... "Three days?"

"Three days!" He stared at her in disbelief. "You did the trip non-stop?"

"I didn't want to waste time—"

"Why didn't you fly?"

"I—"

"Shit. Don't worry about that now. Where's Gavin?"

"Gavin?"

"Yeah, your fiancé, why isn't he here with you?"

"We broke up months ago," she muttered, confused. How could Tris forget that not so insignificant detail?

The bust-up of her engagement was the reason they were in this predicament in the first place.

"He knocked you up and left!" Tris roared.

What? She took a step back. He thought Gavin was the baby daddy? Didn't he think it was strange she was here if Gavin was the father? Did he think she'd drive all this way to tell him she was pregnant with Gavin's kid?

Shaking her head, she said, "Gavin isn't the father."

"What the fuck, Covington?" He moved closer, anger flaring in his eyes. "Tell me who it is and I'll kick the bastard's fucking ass."

He was such an honorable guy. He'd never dream of leaving a woman if he'd gotten her pregnant. Well, he wouldn't leave if he *knew* he'd gotten her pregnant.

Tears stung her eyes and tingled the back of her nose, clogged her throat.

God. It shouldn't be this hard to get the words out.

All she had to say was 'you're the father' but her throat had closed up tight and her chest felt like a band of steel had wrapped around it.

"Aw, Cov." He pulled her into his arms, tucking her head beneath his chin. "It's okay. I promise you, everything will be all right. I'll make sure it is."

He had no idea what he was committing to. "I—" A sob choked off her words, further constricting her chest.

Rubbing his hands up and down her back, he made soothing sounds under his breath and it took every last bit of her remaining energy not to give in to the emotions overwhelming her and completely lose her composure.

It wouldn't be the first time she'd succumbed to a crying jag in the last few months. It wasn't a normal week without her emptying at least one box of tissues.

"Shh... It's okay. You're here now. I'll take care of you," Tris continued to reassure her.

She needed to tell him.

"First thing you need is rest. It couldn't have been easy driving all that way on your own with no break."

Being cradled in Tristan's arms felt wonderful but the idea of lying down, of closing her eyes for longer than the three hour catnaps in her cramped car she'd allowed herself...

Her whole body sagged in longing.

"I'll get my keys and you can take my truck. You're not driving that rattle-trap car anywhere else until I get someone to look at it."

"But—"

"Shh." He tipped her chin up with two fingers and placed his thumb over her lips. "My house is only a short distance down the road. It's easy to find. I've got another sixteen or so hours until my shift ends in the morning then I'll be home. We'll talk about everything then."

"I don't want to put you out."

"You're not."

"I could see about staying—"

"No. You'll stay with me."

"Well, if you're sure, but I can take my car."

"Covington," he growled as he lowered his face to hers, his eyes hard and uncompromising.

She leaned back but his hold prevented her from going too far. "Y-yes."

"Take the fucking truck," he ordered, his jaw clenched.

Opening her mouth to protest, anything she might have managed to say was drowned out by a siren screeching through the building.

"Shit." He let her go. "That's a call. I gotta go."

Tris grabbed her hand and tugged her out of the office and back down the hall before pushing her into another room. This one had two rows of neat bunks and a wall of metal lockers.

He gave her a nudge towards the lockers.

"What?" she asked as she stepped further into the room and glanced over her shoulder at him.

"The locker with my name on it. Grab my keys and meet me out front."

Before Covington could utter a word, Tris was gone. She stood staring at the spot where he'd disappeared, confused and wondering if she should just wait until he returned. But the sound of running feet, shouting and the rumble of a fire engine coming to life snapped her out of her daze.

She found his locker easily enough. The keys were right in front next to his wallet—the one she'd given him last Christmas.

Scooping up the keys, Covington shut the metal door with an unintentionally loud clang and pondered the absence of a lock.

The screeching alarm cut off abruptly and a split second later the wail of a fire engine siren took its place.

Rushing back into the hall, she followed the noise to a large area where several men and the woman from the bathroom were pulling on gear and climbing aboard the two big red trucks.

The garage door had been rolled up and as Tris jumped onto one of the slowly moving fire engines he yelled at her.

"It's the house with the green shutters about five minutes down the road. Eight-ninety-two." He pointed to the right. "Text me when you get there so I know you're safe. I'll call when I can."

Covington followed the trucks as they rolled out of the station. She stood on the driveway watching until they were long gone and the sirens had faded to nothing but a memory.

Glancing at the keys in her hand she thought about the last few minutes.

Seeing Tristan again hadn't gone anything like she thought it would. For one thing, he didn't seem at all angry with her. He'd offered her a place to stay and a reliable vehicle. He'd showed concern and given her comfort, told her everything would be fine.

Promised it would.

And she hadn't told him he was the father of her babies.

Hell, she hadn't actually *told* him she was pregnant, never mind that she was carrying twins and they were his.

CHAPTER 4

TUGGING his vibrating phone from his pocket, Tris looked at the screen and grimaced. Switching the phone off, he ignored Gavin's call for what felt like the millionth time. He thought he'd made himself clear the last time he'd actually answered.

Obviously his former friend chose to ignore his words or Gavin had found out Cov was here.

She'd told him yesterday they weren't together and the baby wasn't Gavin's, and Tris didn't think she would lie about either of those things.

He had no idea if Gavin had been attempting to get back with Cov for real or if he'd been blowing smoke up Tristan's ass for months in the hope of rekindling their friendship.

What Gavin didn't understand or, again, chose to ignore, was that Cov had nothing to do with Tristan severing their friendship.

It was Gavin's actions that had done that. Cov just happened to be the woman Gavin had been engaged to when his ex-friend had shown his true colors.

The phone vibrated in his hand and this time Tris didn't just reject the call, he switched the phone off completely. He wasn't on call and his next shift was two days away.

Plus the only person in his life who might need to get hold of him whom he'd want to talk to was less than a hundred feet away tucked safe inside his house.

Dragging his weary body up the walk to the front door, Tris tried to remember where his Aunt Josie used to hide the spare key. Not that he was even sure it would still be there.

He hadn't bothered to look for it when he'd first taken over the house after her death, and since he'd moved in, he hadn't thought about it because he had the two sets of keys the real estate agent had returned to him.

Lindsey Hogan hadn't been at all disappointed to lose his business when he'd told her he no longer wanted to let the place out as a holiday rental.

When she'd met him at the house three months ago, she'd been exactly as he remembered her from school—in spite of the cool sophistication she'd acquired in adulthood, she was surprisingly still warm and welcoming.

He'd run into her a number of times since then, and she always smiled and asked how he was settling in.

His ex-realtor wasn't the only town member who greeted him with a smile and a chat. Then again, the people of Winter Lake really did want to know how he was doing.

When your aunt was born and bred here and a favored member of the community, you were greeted with acceptance and interest—like family, like you were one of them.

Since the first day he'd returned to Winter Lake, he'd felt at home. It helped that some of the kids—now adults—he'd hung out with in his misspent youth had remained in town.

Devlin, his closest friend then and now, still lived in the house next door.

Which was how he'd gotten home, seeing how the minute they'd returned from the fire yesterday afternoon, he'd called Larry from Lake Auto Repair to come and tow Cov's death-trap of a car to the shop.

Larry had left with the directive to go from bumper to bumper, tires to roof, and write down everything wrong with the old Chevy. No sugar coating either. Tristan wanted to know if the car was salvageable or if he should start looking for something more appropriate—safer—for a future mother.

Larry had looked at the car, a frown marring his brow, and with a shake of his head, muttered, "There ain't no sugar coating *that*," before ambling over to the back of his tow truck.

Tristan was pretty sure he knew what the mechanic would tell him once he'd gone over Cov's car. As much as she loved that vehicle, it was time to let it go.

Reaching the house, he started with the doormat then moved onto the flowerpots lining the porch in search of a key.

Perhaps he should give Cov his truck. It had a dual cab

and four-wheel drive and one of the top safety ratings in the country. Perfect for navigating mountain roads with precious cargo on board.

"Hey."

Glancing up he found Cov standing in the doorway. Waiting.

Straightening, he took her in and smiled.

Jesus, he could get used to that sight.

Especially when she was bundled up in one of his old fire department sweatshirts and a pair of his thick work socks.

The shirt was long on her and she'd pulled the socks up to her knees so only a few inches of her tiger patterned dance leggings showed between the two.

How a woman could look cute as a button and sexy as hell in one go was beyond him, but Cov pulled it off and he was pretty sure she wasn't trying to be either.

One more thing he loved about her, she was completely genuine, none of the fakeness like a lot of the women of his acquaintance in LA where the need to be perfect was often taken to extremes. The fact Cov hadn't succumbed to that trend with the industry she worked in was a miracle.

Grinning, he moved back toward the door and the woman who'd dominated his thoughts for what felt like forever. "Didn't want to ring the bell in case you were sleeping."

She frowned. "It's after midday."

"Is it?" He glanced at his watch, shocked to discover she was right. They'd had a call that took them into change of shift but he hadn't realized it had gotten so late. "No wonder I'm tired."

Fidgeting on her feet and wringing her hands, both nervous actions he hadn't seen in her before, she asked, "Are you hungry? I could make you something for lunch. I hope it's okay I helped myself to some of your food."

"Cov, baby, what's mine is yours. And while I should probably eat, I'm in more need of a shower and sleep. I'll take a rain check though."

"Oh, god." She jumped back, bumping the door wide as she made room for him to enter the house. "It's your house and I've kept you on the doorstep!"

Stepping inside, he chuckled at the fact they'd been having a conversation with him standing outside his own front door. With a shake of his head, he turned toward his room. "I'll grab that shower."

"Um..."

When she didn't continue, he glanced over his shoulder and saw she was shuffling her feet and twisting her hands again.

"What?" he asked as he stopped and turned to face her, giving her his full attention.

"I had to, um, sleep..." She shrugged. "You've only got one bed."

"Oh, yeah. I cleared out all the old furniture when my stuff got here. I haven't set up the other bedrooms yet."

Filling the three-bedroom cottage had been the last thing on his to-do list after his furniture had been delivered. He probably should have kept some of what was in the house when he arrived, but Tris couldn't stand the thought of using what strangers had used.

And he'd yet to go through the shed out back where his mother had stored his aunt's things when he'd first inherited the place and put it up as a rental.

"Tris…"

"Give me a few minutes to shower. We'll talk before I catch some Zs."

Cov nodded. "Okay. Sure." She looked away. "I'll just… make a list of what I ate."

"Jesus. Don't do that." He didn't understand why she was so anxious with him; they'd never been on eggshells around each other but right now Cov looked as though she would shatter if he said boo. "Just put your feet up. I'll be five minutes, tops."

"I should replace—"

"*No,*" he countered with a shake of his head. "You shouldn't."

Before she could come up with another argument or something else to delay his shower, he strode down the hall and into the bathroom.

He knew they had things to discuss. Firstly, he wanted to know what she was doing here—why had she come to him? Then he wanted to know the name of the asshole who had knocked her up and left her to deal with the baby alone.

Not that *who* really mattered. Tris would step up for her and the baby.

He'd made that decision while lying sleepless in his

bunk last night. He didn't care who had fathered her baby; he would make sure neither of them went without.

As the child of a single mother, Tristan had seen first-hand how hard things could be. He didn't want that for Covington. Or her child.

Between now and when the baby came, he'd convince Cov to marry him and put his name on the birth certificate under father.

It was the best option for both of them.

He could provide a safe place for them to live as well as healthcare. He had no idea if Cov had her own insurance, but he doubted it.

For as long as he'd known her, she'd only had the one long-term job and that had been a six-month contract, not exactly a permanent job or regular income.

He also had no idea how much she earned. Did she get paid per job or per hour? Did she have savings?

And what would happen now she was pregnant?

He didn't think there would be much demand for pregnant dancers and as far as he knew Cov didn't have any other qualifications.

Shucking his sweatpants and briefs, he reached into the shower stall and turned on the water.

The hot took forever to come through the old pipes and as much as he needed a wake up, he could do without freezing his nuts off.

The temp had dropped overnight to its lowest point this fall and the house was on the chilly side already.

He'd have to check the thermostat and furnace after he cleaned up.

He didn't want Cov getting cold. With her thin LA blood, she was probably half frozen even though the temps had been quite warm for this time of year. Until now anyway.

And there was more cold weather coming according to the forecast. They were in for the first big snow dump of the season in three days. Right in the middle of his next shift.

He would have to make sure Cov had everything she needed before his forty-eight hour rotation began. He hated the thought of her attempting to navigate the snow-covered roads.

Actually, now that he thought about it, he didn't think she'd ever seen snow before.

Jesus. It was a wonder she'd made it here at all. Between her death-trap of a car and the snow-covered roads, her arriving safe and sound was a miracle.

The thought of everything that could have gone wrong had him shuddering.

Steam rose as he yanked off his shirt and stepped under the spray. He'd be quick in spite of his desire to linger.

Now that he'd made up his mind about what they should do, he wanted to move forward with his plan. He had a lot to organize before he went back to work Saturday morning.

Cov would need a winter jacket and boots to start. He hadn't seen either on her or in her car and she would never make it through winter without them. They needed to get her prepared for the cold months ahead.

He'd have to ask her about the rest of her stuff. Had she packed up her apartment?

He hadn't looked in the trunk of her car and there hadn't been a suitcase or boxes on the backseat…

Had she brought anything besides the clothes on her back with her? He knew by the tag still attached she'd bought her gloves somewhere along the way—probably the scarves too.

Why had she undertaken such a long, hard journey without being prepared?

So many questions.

It didn't matter. She'd come to him and he had to believe she'd done so because she needed his help —wanted it.

Maybe it was the 'hero complex' his mother accused him of having, but Tristan felt it was his job to make sure Cov was okay. More than okay.

He wanted her to have everything she needed— anything she wanted.

And if that meant marrying her and being a father to her unborn child then he'd gladly step up and do it.

CHAPTER 5

C OVINGTON HADN'T BEEN able to put her feet up as Tris directed.

She was like a kid on a sugar high bouncing around from room to room, not able to sit for more than a few seconds.

Dancing had always been her mode of coping with stress or anxiety, and she had plenty of both going on right now.

Unfortunately her go-to release valve was no longer an option because she'd completely lost her balance and rhythm since she'd fallen pregnant.

So now she walked.

Or fidgeted.

Or twitched.

It seemed the babies didn't only hijack her hormones, they'd hijacked her nervous system too. And her brain. They'd rewired that somehow.

All around, she felt like one big pregnant idiot.

Why else would she sell everything she owned and drive over three thousand miles with nowhere to live?

Funny how she hadn't questioned her decision until she'd driven out of LA just after sunrise at the start of the week.

Actually, it wasn't until she'd crossed into Pennsylvania that she had started to second-guess her choices, and by then it was far too late to turn back, so she had sucked it up and kept going.

For the rest of the way she'd been on tenterhooks, and that nerve-wracking anxiety hadn't lessened in spite of Tristan's warm welcome and offer of accommodation.

It probably didn't help that she still hadn't told him the babies were his.

She'd been working up the nerve to reveal his part in her 'condition' since she let herself into his house last night.

Of course she'd gotten a little distracted when she'd fallen into his bed. The soft sheets smelled like him and suddenly she had other things on her mind.

Snuggling in, she had spent half the night reminiscing, the other half dreaming.

Her memories—and dreams—of their one night together were so vivid that when she had woken this morning, she'd thought the last four months hadn't happened, that she hadn't kicked Tris out of her bed, and rolled over with a smile that had died on her lips when she discovered the space beside her empty.

The pillow undented by Tristan's head.

All the anxiety that had disappeared in the comfort of Tris's bed had come rushing back. The deluge would have crippled her if she hadn't already been lying down.

And typical of recent weeks, the waterworks had started—the ones in her eyes and the one between her legs—and she'd cried her way to the bathroom and gone through a whole roll of toilet paper.

The man didn't skimp on toilet paper, thank goodness, because he certainly didn't buy tissues. There wasn't a box in the house. She knew because she'd searched.

He didn't really have much and while the house was warm and comfy, it didn't quite feel lived in. Then again, he hadn't been here long; if her information was right, he only moved in three months ago.

Even with the bareness of the rooms—two of them completely empty—the place still felt like his. She could feel him in every room. It helped take the edge off her nerves.

Amazing how until now she'd never noticed how much Tristan's presence settled her. Well, when she wasn't stressing over telling him he was going to be a dad anyway.

Although if she were honest, her stress levels had changed ever since she'd set eyes on him yesterday.

Yes, she was worried about his reaction to their impending parenthood, but if she dug deep, really looked at it, she knew he'd stand by her; it was the reason he'd do it that had her concerned.

She wanted his help because he wanted to help *her*, not only because he'd knocked her up.

Which was stupid because if he hadn't knocked her up she wouldn't need his help.

Sighing, she stared at the list she'd put together. If she concentrated on what they needed, her mind might stop spinning in circles around things she had no way of predicting or fixing on her own.

A shopping list she could deal with.

Right on top were tissues, then eggs and milk and cheese. Fruit and veggies and meat.

Tris had a well-stocked pantry but his fresh produce was minimal and she needed to keep her diet balanced or she risked her and the babies' health.

Her pregnancy might be completely unexpected, but Covington wasn't about to put the babies in danger. Especially when she'd lost so much weight in the first few weeks. She needed to be sure she looked after all three of them from now on.

Building herself back up while building babies took more food than she was used to eating but it wasn't as though she needed to keep herself in peak physical form for dancing at the moment.

She'd been fooling herself thinking she could continue to dance for a living until she gave birth—for now and the foreseeable future she was unemployable in her chosen profession.

She could afford to overindulge a little between now and when she could return to work.

The one thing she had to do was stop giving in to her cravings for junk food. She'd consumed far too much sugar and fat in recent days.

It was only that she'd barely been able to keep down her own spit for all those weeks that she'd eaten anything and everything she felt like since the morning sickness had eased in the last week or so.

Although today she hadn't been able to stomach the thought of food never mind actually eating. The churning in her belly wasn't the usual pregnancy nausea though.

No, the urge to vomit lay solely at the feet of her anxiety about telling Tristan he was going to be a father.

Times two.

In five months.

Probably less.

Twins often arrived early. She knew that. She'd read it in one of the pamphlets the nurse at the doctor's office had given her on her last visit.

"Hey, I thought I told you to put your feet up."

Tris entered the kitchen in a pair of sweats riding low on his hips, the deep V cutting through the sides of his lower torso making her fingers tingle to explore.

His chest was bare, the dusting of dark hair across his pecs sparkling with a few missed droplets of water, and she had to stop herself from stepping forward and cleaning those up for him.

Her gaze traveled over every inch of naked flesh with unbridled pleasure. Heat rushed through her, and Covington swallowed the little whimper of desire that worked its way up her throat.

She remembered licking that chest. Remembered weaving her fingers through the hair, scraping her nails over his nipples. And remembered licking her way down his stomach, her tongue trailing a wet path through those deep trenches leading to his pulsing...

"Covington."

Her gaze snapped up, colliding with Tristan's heated one, and a shiver vibrated along her spine in the wake of the low, dark rumble of his voice, the hunger swirling in his eyes.

She licked her lips, pushed her lusting thoughts aside, and tried to focus on what had to be done. "W-we should talk."

Clearing his throat, he nodded. "Yeah, we should." He stepped closer and every nerve in her body buzzed, went on high alert.

Oh, who was she kidding? The man had her on high alert all the damn time. She only had to think of him to be a puddle of lust-laced goo.

Or it was pregnancy hormones.

Hormones went berserk during pregnancy. She'd read that in one of the handouts too.

Yes. That was it. She wanted to lick Tris all over because her hormones were in overdrive.

Times two.

Probably.

Hopefully.

Lord, if it wasn't the pregnancy...

"Are you okay?"

She blinked. "Huh?"

"You look a little flushed and your eyes are glassy and dilated." He leaned forward, his gaze searching her face as he placed the back of his hand on her forehead. "I think you should sit down. You feel clammy, a bit warm."

Clammy? A bit warm?

Ha!

Right now she was sweating. She hadn't done that since before she'd driven up into the mountains.

Shaking away his hand, she pushed those pesky hormones aside as well, and attempted to behave like a sensible human being, not a seething mass of lust.

"I'm fine. Pregnancy raises a woman's temperature." She'd read that somewhere too. Those leaflets were a goldmine of information.

"Oh, right. About that."

This was it. The perfect time to tell him about the babies.

"I need to tell you something."

Her voice came out little more than a whisper, a bit shaky with the anxiety squeezing her throat.

He nodded, one corner of his mouth tipping up in an encouraging smile. "Okay."

"I'm pregnant."

Tris chuckled. "Yeah, I got that."

"Right. Well, I'm having twins—"

"We should get married," he cut in.

"And they're...*what? Married?*"

"Twins!"

They talked over the top of each other.

"*Married?* No. We can't get married." She shook her head frantically.

"There's two in there?"

"Are you insane?"

"Two?" He stared wide-eyed at her stomach. "Seriously. You've got two in there?"

"Stop. Stop. Stop. Stop." Covington held up her hands, resisted the urge to stick her fingers in her ears and sing *lah-lah-lah-lah-lah*... "Stop talking. Just for a minute. Stop talking. I need a minute."

She needed to wrap her head around the conversation. Her brain hadn't been in the best of order since she'd gotten pregnant and honestly she needed a minute—or fifty million—to get over the fact that Tristan Harding just offered to marry her.

And he didn't even know the babies were his!

Spinning on her socked foot, she headed for the living room. "I need to sit." Possibly lie down.

"Are you okay?" He gripped her elbow, steering her in the direction she was already going but with a little more speed. "Do you need a doctor? Should you be walking around? You're not in labor, are you?"

She could hear the panic escalating in his voice. The big, tough firefighter who ran into burning buildings for a living was freaking out over a pregnant woman.

She rolled her eyes.

Great. That's exactly what they needed. Two of them freaking out. Poor babies. Her hand slid over her belly.

I promise we'll get it together when it counts.

"I'm fine. Just need to sit." *Put my head between my legs.*

She didn't say the last part for fear he'd really freak out on her.

He pushed her onto the couch, grabbed her feet, and

swung her legs up as he pressed on her shoulder so she was stretched out along the seat cushions, her head resting against the arm.

Crouching down beside her, he held her hand with both of his. "Tell me what to do. What do you need? Should I call someone?"

It was probably the wrong thing to do but she couldn't stop the bubble of laughter that burst out of her. The whole situation was hilarious.

Okay, maybe not, but she'd been inside out and upside down for months now and if she wasn't laughing, she'd probably be crying, and she hadn't bought tissues yet and...

A hiccup squeezed her middle and jolted her chest.

Her nose tingled and her eyes stung.

Her throat tightened.

Then she made a noise that was a cross between a laugh and a sob and possibly a dying animal and no matter what she wanted or didn't want, there was no stopping the jag taking her over.

Through blurry eyes she saw Tristan's horrified face and cried harder.

She'd never been one of those pretty criers either.

Nope. She was all puffy eyes and red nose.

Big fat tears and snot.

Lots and lots of snot.

If she wasn't so out of control, she'd be horrified that Tris was seeing her like this.

"Shh, shh, shh," Tris soothed as he pulled her into his arms, cradled her against his chest, and tucked her face into the warm curve of his neck. "It'll be okay. You'll be fine. The babies will be fine. I promise. *Everything* will be fine."

She sobbed against his skin, covering both of them with tears and snot and making a mess of everything.

God. She used to be so in control. Independent. Self-reliant. And now she was clinging to a man who had no idea he'd gotten her pregnant with twins but wanted to marry her anyway.

CHAPTER 6

Tris held Cov close and ignored the warm, slimy stuff sliding down his chest.

One thing he'd always admired about Covington was her enthusiasm. Anything she did, she did with all her heart. It seemed crying her heart out was no exception.

Holding her as tight as he dared, he concentrated on not demanding answers to the questions swirling in his head.

She didn't appear to be in physical pain and while she hadn't denied being in labor when he asked, he was pretty sure she wasn't.

God, he hoped she wasn't.

He wasn't prepared for that yet.

He would be. He'd have to be. But for now he just had to be a shoulder to cry on.

Someone she could depend on. A friend.

A smile curled one end of his mouth as more liquid slid down his chest. And possibly a sponge.

The longer she cried, the wetter they both got but he didn't care.

Covington Valenti was in his arms and even if she appeared to be falling to pieces he didn't care. She was in. His. Arms.

He'd put her back together or help her put herself together. He'd hold her hand or stand beside her. Whatever she needed, he'd provide.

He was more than likely in for a world of hurt because there was no denying how he felt about the woman in his arms.

But now wasn't the time to deal with his emotions. Cov and the babies were his priority. He'd be here for all three of them; no matter what happened, she'd always be able to count on him.

They would always be able to.

Her sobs tapered off, each one less body-wracking than the last and he just kept on holding her, kept on soothing her with nonsense words and whispered promises he'd keep 'til his dying breath.

He had no idea how long they stayed there, him on his knees, her half on the couch, half in his lap, before Cov's breathing evened out and her tears appeared to stop.

It was a few more minutes, the occasional hitched sob, and a couple of deep breaths before she broke the silence.

"S-sorry," she sputtered into his wet neck. He was pretty sure a bubble of something just popped against his skin.

"It's okay." And strangely it was. He didn't care that she'd covered him with body fluid. He'd prefer a different kind but he'd take anything she gave him. He'd take her tears and her smiles and everything in between. He held her tighter and waited until her body relaxed completely. "Feel better?"

She nodded smearing the mess between them further.

He smoothed his hands up and down her back. "Want to tell me what brought that on?"

"Hormones?"

"Ah, okay..." That certainly cleared things up. Not. He had some reading to do.

"I swear, it's like I've got a split personality or something. One minute I'm smiling and the next I'm leaking all over the place."

"So we don't need to find a doctor?" He was worried she needed medical attention. His experience with pregnant women could be counted in minutes. All of them with her.

"No." She brought her arm up between her body and his and tried to clean both of them with the sleeve of her borrowed sweatshirt. "I've covered us in goop."

He smiled into her hair. "Not the first time I've been covered in goop."

She tipped her head back and stared up at him with blotchy cheeks and puffy, red-rimmed eyes. "Women cry all over you all the time?"

"Well, no. You'd be the first. But there's plenty of goop in my line of work."

She swiped her sleeve across his neck again. The fabric,

already saturated, did nothing but smear the slick mess more. "Ah...um. Maybe you should shower again," she murmured, a frown creasing her brow.

"Let's get you fixed up first." Tris stood, picking her up with ease. She wasn't as heavy as he remembered and he knew women hated to talk about their weight but shouldn't she be bigger now she was having a baby? *Babies.* Jesus. He had to get his head around that. "Have you seen a doctor?"

"Yes." She covered a yawn with her hand. "Back home."

"And everything is okay?" She felt fragile in his arms and she'd gone to pieces a minute ago, which to his mind said things weren't normal. Then again, what would he know and *two* babies.

"Yes. I lost some weight early on because of morning sickness but everything's progressing like it should otherwise. The babies are growing like they should." She snuggled into him and used her clean sleeve to wipe her face as he walked down the hall.

"And you're staying? Here? With me?" He wanted to be sure he got her agreement on that right now.

"If it's okay?" Her words slurred a little, her eyes drifting closed as her breathing deepened, lost the last of the hiccupy sobs.

"Definitely." He didn't add that he'd track her down and haul her back if she left.

She was obviously wiped out from crying and he doubted she'd caught up after the long drive to reach him because by the time he arrived in his bedroom, Cov was sound asleep, her head slumped against his shoulder, the cutest little snore slipping through her lips with each breath.

Easing her onto the unmade bed, he debated removing the wet sweatshirt. The house was warmer since he'd upped the thermostat after his shower but he didn't want to risk her getting cold. It couldn't be comfortable having all that wet fabric sticking to her skin either.

With as much care as he could manage, he pulled the top off and tucked her under the covers without waking her.

Using the body of the sweatshirt, he cleaned her face as best he could. She stirred. Mumbled something about needing to tell the babies' daddy and tissues.

Tris shook his head and smiled. He had no idea what one had to do with the other. It didn't matter. Right now she needed rest and he had less than forty-eight hours before his next shift to make sure she got plenty of it.

After her nap, they'd head out to get some groceries. They needed to stock up and get ready for the big snowfall heading their way.

They should probably see about getting an appointment with a doctor too.

He believed her when she said everything was fine, but for his peace of mind he'd like Jared Groves to take a look at her, plus she'd need a doctor to see her through the rest of her pregnancy.

Like Tristan, the doc was new in town, but unlike Tristan, Jared Groves had never set foot in Winter Lake before taking over the town's one and only medical facility.

Tris had liked the doctor instantly and, more importantly, he trusted him. Putting Cov and her babies in the other man's capable hands felt right.

Yeah, they'd definitely make an appointment before he went back on shift.

Leaving the bedroom and a sleeping Cov, he went to the bathroom, cleaned himself up quickly and grabbed the dirty wash. He'd put a load on now, then he could toss it in the dryer before they went shopping.

Depending on how long she slept, he'd suggest stopping for an early dinner at Della's Dina first. They could both do with a good hot meal, and there was nothing better than the comfort food that came out of Della's kitchen.

With the clothes in the washer, he went back to check on Cov. She was right where he'd left her. Tucked up in his bed, curled beneath his covers. He couldn't resist the urge to lie down beside her and watch her sleep.

Taking his time so he didn't disturb her, he eased onto the bed next to her. With his head on one hand, he fisted the other behind his back to stop himself from reaching out and touching her.

Her face was thinner, and the dark smudges under her eyes had to go. She looked different but the same. There were subtle changes but she was still beautiful. He hadn't seen her smile yet.

He'd lived for those smiles even when she'd been engaged to another man.

From the minute he'd met her, Tris hadn't been able to stop himself from getting close to her—from falling for her.

It had taken some serious willpower to not touch her in

all the months he'd known her. He wasn't surprised he'd caved into the need the second the one thing standing in his way had been removed.

Of course now he wasn't sure that had been the best move. Look how that turned out.

He'd heard people talk about a rebound fuck and honestly, he'd never thought he'd find himself on the end of one of those. Especially with the woman he'd wanted from the second he'd met her.

He thought they'd been on the same page, fighting an attraction that couldn't be while she was promised to another man, but then he'd known the truth about that man and she had finally seen it and the rest, as they say, was history.

They'd been combustible from the first touch. He hadn't really been surprised by their chemistry; it was the connection he'd felt while they were together that he hadn't believed could only be on his side.

Except the morning after proved otherwise; her words had sliced through any fantasies he'd had of them finally being together.

Tris had left LA believing his chance to be with Covington had been ruined because he'd rushed. If he'd just given her time to get over Gavin's betrayal, things might have turned out differently for them.

If he'd been able to control himself they might not have gone up in flames. He might not have moved to Winter Lake to lick his wounds. To start a life without her in it.

Except now she was here.

In his house.

In his bed.

Pregnant with someone else's babies and he didn't give a damn. He still wanted her.

The sweatshirt had hidden her belly but when he'd removed it he'd seen the swell beneath her t-shirt.

He'd never thought about having children. They hadn't been on his radar. Now, after seeing the gentle curve of her body that cradled two miracles of life, it was all he could think about.

He wanted those babies to be his. Wanted to have that connection with her for the rest of their lives. He'd been half in love with her before.

She'd driven him almost out of his mind until he'd gotten a taste of her and he'd known his life would never be the same.

He'd wanted to deepen their friendship from the beginning. The idea he'd ruined it completely had sent him across the country; he hadn't thought there was any hope for them after her parting words and his tuck-tailed run to Winter Lake, but now here she was.

Sleeping beside him.

Pregnant.

And all he could think about was pulling her close and holding on.

Never letting her go.

CHAPTER 7

Covington's gaze darted around the room taking in the mismatched tablecloths, the shelves covered in knick-knacks, the various photo frames hanging on the timber walls. In spite of the biting cold wind that followed them inside, she felt instantly warm, as though someone had walked over and wrapped her up in a welcoming hug.

The place had so much character. So much *life*. There were plenty of places in LA with both of those but Covington had never felt so at home before. Not even in her apartment had she felt this instantly relaxed.

Smiling, she turned to Tris. "I love it! It's so...comfortable."

"You want comfort? Wait until you taste the food." Putting a hand on her lower back, he steered her toward a table near the window. "Nothing and nobody beats Della's Dina for comfort food."

She slid into the chair Tris pulled out as a grandmotherly woman with a beaming smile hurried their way. "Good to see you, Tristan. And who do we have here?" she asked as she handed Covington a menu.

Tris smiled and made introductions. "Della, this is Covington. Cov, Della, the genius behind this fine establishment."

The older woman smiled at her and said, "She's prettier than your usual companion, Tristan."

"I have to agree with you, Della." Tris grinned. "Although perhaps we shouldn't tell Devlin. Wouldn't want to bruise his fragile ego."

Della laughed. "That boy's ego could do with a little bruising if you ask me."

Tris held up his hands. "I'm not getting into that discussion."

The door opened with a whoosh of cold air, drawing Della's gaze. "Oh. I'll be right back. My grandson and his wife just came in."

Covington watched as Della expertly wove her way through tables to the front door where the two people who had entered were removing their bulky jackets and scarves. They were easily recognizable in spite of their winter layers.

Kirby Swan and Race Parker.

Cov leaned forward, her gaze still on the new arrivals, and whispered in disbelief, *"Race Parker is her grandson?"*

"Yes. Do you know him?"

Her gaze swung to Tris. "Know him? Everyone knows who Race Parker is. And don't get me started on how legendary Kirby Swan is."

"Oh, right, you mean because they're famous. I always forget that. They're just Race and Kirby around here."

"They're just..." She stared at Tris, her mouth hanging open.

To prove his point, Tris lifted his hand and waved. "Hey, Race. Kirby."

Covington snapped her mouth closed and gripped the edges of her seat.

"Hi, Tristan. You get that furnace at Miss Josie's fixed yet?" Race asked as he headed their way.

"Yep, ripped it out. Decided not to risk another breakdown and installed a new one instead of repairing the outdated model."

"Probably wise. I remember when Josie had that old one put in," Della added. "Jack Peters did the job the year before he had his heart attack. Gosh, that must be a good twenty years ago now."

"Do I know you from somewhere?"

Covington's gaze zipped to the side, her eyes going wide and her stomach dipping low when she found Kirby Swan studying her with interest. "I...um..."

"Kirby, Race, this is Covington Valenti."

Race smiled down at her. "Nice to meet you."

"Covington's an unusual name. I'd remember that if we'd met before. I could swear I know you though." Kirby offered her hand. "Welcome to Winter Lake."

Reflexes had Covington taking the superstar singer's hand. "T-thank you."

"Cov's a dancer. Maybe you two have worked together before," Tris offered.

"No!" Covington blurted, shaking her head. "We haven't worked together."

A strained silence followed her outburst and the comfort she'd felt moments ago vanished under a wave of embarrassment.

Race broke the awkward moment. "Well, we'll let you get back to it."

Kirby smiled and said, "Lovely to meet you," before Race took her elbow and guided her toward the doorway at the back of the café.

"See. Just Race and Kirby," Tris said with a grin.

Covington pulled her eyes away from the disappearing duo and shook her head. "Sorry. There isn't anything *just* about either one of them."

"You two need a few more minutes to decide what you want?" Della asked.

"Oh." Covington jumped. She'd forgotten the other woman was there.

Her mind had been taken over by two of the country's most famous singers. One of whom was this woman's grandson. Way to make an impression.

In an attempt to appear less like a star-struck idiot and more like a completely sane customer, she asked. "What would you recommend?"

"Depends on how hungry you are. Tristan here always has the pot roast with extra potato and gravy."

Tris chuckled. "You know me well."

"That sounds good. I'll have that too." Covington smiled and held out the menu. "And a glass of milk."

"Your usual iced tea, Tristan?" At his nod Della took the

menu from Covington and confirmed their order. "Glass of milk, iced tea, and two roasts coming right up."

After Della walked away Covington bent over and pressed her forehead against the table. Barely resisted the urge to thump her head on the hard surface. "Oh my god, I'm a complete idiot," she muttered into the tablecloth.

"What makes you say that?" Tris wedged his hand between her head and the table.

Tipping her face up, she gazed at him with astonishment. "Are you serious? I just made a fool of myself because I couldn't get over the fact Kirby Swan and Race Parker weren't just breathing the same air as me, they were *talking* to me."

Tris laughed. "I'm sure you're not the first to get a little tongue tied."

"I wish my tongue *had* been tied."

"You weren't that bad." He chucked her under the chin. "Don't worry about it. Here come our drinks."

At the mention of fluid, a spasm gripped her bladder and she sat up straight, squeezing her legs together. "Oh."

Tris frowned at her. "What?"

"I have to pee," she whispered.

Grinning, he pointed in the direction Kirby and Race had gone. "That way."

"Thanks." Tightening her muscles, Covington waited until she was sure there would be no risk of leakage before she stood and dashed between tables and into the hallway.

She found the restroom and pushed inside almost taking out the woman coming out. "Sorry," she called out as she rushed into the cubicle without looking back.

There were many things about being pregnant that Covington had discovered weren't all *glowing*. One was her new toileting habit. No warning and no time to wait.

In the beginning she'd been caught out a number of times. Even had to go so far as to carry a spare pair of panties in her handbag.

Although she'd managed to avoid using them up until now, you could bet the minute she stopped carrying them around she'd be back to peeing her pants.

The information leaflets might have mentioned the whole need-to-pee-every-other-second phenomenon, but they failed to explain the embarrassing side effects.

Those she'd learned about firsthand, and after having had to purchase new underwear twice, Covington had wised-up and come prepared from then on.

Relief flowed out of her as coiled muscles unwound and the call of nature was answered.

God. In the last few weeks, peeing had taken the place of sex on the top of her list of best feelings ever.

Except that one night with Tris. *That* was the best feeling ever.

Which was sad when she thought about it. Sad that she'd only had one night, and sad that before him, she'd actually believed she knew what good sex was.

"You okay?"

Jolting on the seat, she threw out her hands, palms flat on the walls either side of her, and was thankful her naked ass didn't end up on the floor.

Kirby Swan wanted to know if she was okay? Had it been Kirby she'd almost bowled over coming in here?

"Are you sick? Do you need help?" Kirby asked.

"N-no. I'm fine."

What was with all these women asking her if she needed help to pee?

Okay, fine, two women, but still, did she look as out of control as she felt?

Covington waited for the sound of footsteps or a door opening but heard nothing except her own harsh breathing.

Why was she freaking out?

Sure, she'd idolized Kirby Swan for years, tried twice to get on the troop of dancers who toured with the singer and had dreamed about working with her, but it wasn't like she was auditioning *now*.

Except first impressions and all that...

She sighed.

She'd be forever known as the crazy pregnant woman in the restroom at Della's Dina.

Necessities taken care of, Covington tugged up her pants and thanked the cold weather for requiring bulky sweaters.

The one she'd borrowed from Tris came to mid-thigh and hid the fact the pants she had on no longer reached around her middle and therefore sat precariously low on her hips.

Good thing she'd grown an ass as well as a belly. That extra booty gave her pants something to hang on to.

"Going to have to bite the bullet and buy new clothes," she muttered as she opened the stall door.

"What was that?"

"Argh!" Covington stumbled backwards, lost her footing, and landed on the toilet.

Thank god she'd closed the lid.

"Sorry." Kirby reached out a hand. "Didn't mean to scare you."

"Oh, you didn't..." She smiled. "Okay, you did."

Taking the offered hand, Covington got to her feet and tried to pretend it wasn't *the* Kirby Swan helping her up.

"Thanks." Letting go of the singer's hand, she moved past her to the basin and cringed at the thought of having touched Kirby Swan without washing her hands first.

Did she point that out?

Apologize?

Suggest she wash her hands too?

"Blair Carmichael's *White Lace*."

"What?" Covington's gaze snapped up to meet Kirby's in the mirror.

"You were the lead dancer in the video."

"Oh. Yes. That was me."

"I knew it! I never forget a face. I might not have known your name but I definitely remember your moves," Kirby explained with a grin.

Covington frowned. She'd worked on that clip the week before she'd found Gavin in bed with another woman.

It was her best work, even if she said so herself, and that lying cheating jerk had ruined it for her by being a douche.

They'd wrapped early and she'd headed to Gavin's to tell him about the bonus she'd gotten only to find him in bed with Steffii—*double f, double i*—the bulimic chick she'd beaten for the lead part in the video.

She still couldn't understand why she hadn't seen Gavin's true colors before that day. When she looked back now, it was like red flashing lights going off the whole time.

God. She'd even let him talk her out of suspecting him of anything when she'd found a pair of panties in the wash that weren't hers.

Somehow he'd convinced her she must have picked them up with her gear at the club she danced at two nights a week.

Can you say gullible?

How about stupid?

"Hey. You okay?" Kirby moved in beside her, placing a hand on her shoulder. "You've gone a little pale."

"Hmm... Oh, sorry. Bad memories." At the look of horror on Kirby's face, Covington rushed to explain. "Not of Blair or the video. Other stuff—personal stuff—I'd rather forget about that happened during the shoot."

"Oh. Sorry I brought it up then."

"No. No, it's all right." She shrugged. "I shouldn't connect one with the other. It really was a great video and Blair is a sweetheart." Not to mention hotter than hot and the country's latest pin-up hunk.

Although for all his gorgeousness, he hadn't done it for her. The only one to manage that was Tristan, which said an awful lot about her relationship with Gavin.

Something to ponder at a later time for sure.

Right now she should get back to Tris before he sent in a search party or came looking for her himself.

"I should get back to..."

"Oh, right." Kirby smiled. "Listen. This might seem strange but would you be interested in joining me and some of my friends at a book club? It's nothing formal or anything. And really, it's more of a wine and gossip club, but it's fun and I'd love the chance to talk to you more."

"I, um, *really*?" Why would Kirby Swan invite a virtual stranger to her book club?

"Of course. We're always adding to the ranks and I bet Terra will want to ask questions about the choreography of the White Lace video."

"Well..."

"You don't have to decide now. I'll write down the details so if you want to come, you know where and when. We're at Lindsey's this week."

"Lindsey?"

"One of the original members of the Books and Bitches book club and one of my closest BFFs. You'll like her. Everyone does." Kirby grinned and opened the door. "I'll duck into the office and scribble down the details for you."

"Thanks." What else could she say? It wasn't every day she got to hang out with Kirby Swan.

Hell, it wasn't *any* day. She wanted to laugh at the absurdity of the whole situation.

"I'll think about it and let you know."

"Sure thing."

They entered the hallway and paused, Covington's back to the restaurant. "Thanks again, for the invite."

"You're welcome. How far are you?" Kirby asked, gesturing to Covington's slightly rounded belly.

"Four months."

"Only four?" Kirby's face scrunched up as she realized what those two words implied. "Ah...I mean..."

Covington laughed. "Don't worry. It's twins. I'm told I'll be bigger than a house before they're born."

"Twins? Wow. You'll have your hands full. Good thing Tristan is more than capable of handling things. He'll be a great father."

Smiling, Covington nodded. "Yeah, he's going to be the best."

"Cov?"

Air rushed through her lips as she sucked in a breath. Closing her eyes, she whispered, "He's behind me, isn't he?"

Keeping one eye squeezed shut, Covington cracked the other to find Kirby nodding at her, a smile of sympathy on her face.

Taking a deep breath, she opened her other eye and smiled. "I'll let you know about the book club."

"Sure. No pressure. I'll bring you the details before you leave."

Covington watched as Kirby turned and walked away, disappearing into what she assumed was an office.

Taking another deep breath, this one filled with fear and shame and hope, she spun around and faced Tristan.

CHAPTER 8

Tris didn't know what to think or feel or do.

He stared at the woman who'd kept him awake more nights than any firehouse shift and wondered why the fuck he hadn't thought *he* could be responsible for the babies in her belly.

Jesus Christ.

His babies!

"I'm sorry." Cov reached out a hand but lowered it before she touched him.

"I'm not." He stepped forward and grabbed her retreating hand, squeezing it gently. "I'll never be sorry about anything that's happened between us."

"I..." She swallowed, her eyes going glassy. "I didn't know where you were."

Shit. He'd left her. Spent the night with her then left town never to be seen again.

It didn't matter that they'd used protection and there

shouldn't have been consequences; there were, and the babies were the least of those.

God.

They had history—a relationship—and he'd turned his back on it all because of a few words she'd said while in an emotionally raw state.

He'd been an ass. He was the one who should be apologizing.

"I lied. I'm sorry for one thing." He couldn't resist pulling her into his arms. "I should never have left you."

"You didn't have any reason to stay." She sniffled against his chest and he hoped they weren't about to have a repeat of this morning's messy meltdown.

"I had plenty of reasons to stay." He wanted to tell her how he felt but he wasn't about to get into their complicated relationship in the back of Della's where anyone could listen in.

They'd be fuel for the gossip mill soon enough.

Hell, they probably already were.

Cov had been in town since yesterday. Everyone and their mother would know about Tristan Harding's pregnant visitor by now.

It explained why Della hadn't batted an eye at seeing him with a woman.

Cov tried to pull out of his arms, but he held tight for a moment longer.

Sighing, she relaxed against him. "We should talk about—"

"Not now. Food first, then shopping, then home."

Plus he needed time to think. And another moment of her in his arms.

"Why aren't you angry?" she asked against his shoulder.

Good question.

There might be some anger swirling around in the kaleidoscope of emotions currently tangled inside him but it wasn't at her.

Nope.

That was aimed squarely at himself for letting his wounded pride keep him from going back after she'd thrown him out.

"There's nothing to be angry about. You've done nothing wrong."

"I didn't tell you," she argued.

"And you didn't know where I was." Dumbass that he was, he'd made sure of that. "What did you do when you found out I was in Winter Lake?"

"I packed up as quickly as I could and came here."

Tristan smiled, dropped a kiss on the top of her head, and finally loosened his hold. "You think about that and let me know if you still believe I have reason to be angry about not knowing before now."

"I should have at least called."

"And told me over the phone? No." He shook his head. "Not your style."

"Still."

"No. You haven't done anything to hide this from me. If anything, I hid from you and for that I'm so fucking sorry. Sorry I wasn't there when you found out. Sorry I wasn't there to hold your hair back when the babies made you sick. Sorry you had to drive thousands of miles in only a few days to find me."

"I don't understand you." She pulled away and wiped her nose with the back of her hand. "I didn't exactly tell *you* you're the father."

"I am though, right?"

Suddenly he needed the words. Needed to hear her say those babies were his while looking him in the eyes.

"Yes, they're yours. You're the only man I've been with in ten months." She ducked her head.

"What?" That couldn't be right. She'd been engaged to Gavin...

That fucking asshole. If ever he showed his face in front of Tris again, he'd find it full of fist.

She sniffed and rubbed her nose again. "Gavin wasn't interested."

Fist followed by fist followed by foot.

"That fucker," he growled under his breath.

"It wasn't Gavin's fault."

"Yes, it was." He clenched his jaw. Ground his teeth.

She didn't need to see his anger over the whole Gavin situation. Pulling it in, he reminded himself they had better things to discuss than her ex-fiancé and his ex-friend.

"I don't want to get into that now." Or ever really. As far as he was concerned, they could put Gavin firmly in the past and move on from here. The two of them. Shit. *Four.* The four of them.

Cov glanced around them, said, "Oh," as if she'd

completely forgotten where they were, making him smile and tug on her hand.

"C'mon. Della will get upset if we let our dinner go cold."

She sniffled again as her stomach let loose with a rumbling growl.

Tris laughed. "I think our babies are hungry."

Her hand jerked in his and he tightened his grip in case she thought about letting go.

"Everything will be fine," he vowed. And it would be. He'd make sure of it.

Why he felt the need to reassure her he didn't know, but the urge was too potent to resist. Then again, maybe he was the one in need of verbal reassurance. At this point, he wasn't sure how to untangle the chaotic emotions tugging at him.

One thing he did know now that he knew those babies were his, he was definitely putting a ring on her finger.

The sooner the better.

How long did it take to get a license? Didn't they need blood tests or something?

He'd have to Google it later. After he'd seen to Cov.

She'd spent four months dealing with her pregnancy alone. There would be no more of that.

From now on, he would be with her every step of the way.

Which led him back to their need to find a doctor.

"We should stop by the clinic after here. See about getting in to see Jared Groves before I go back on shift."

"I saw my doctor just before I left LA."

"I'd still like you to see Jared." He *needed* her to see him.

"Well, I do have to find someone to take over my care but there isn't any rush."

She might not think so, and a qualified medical practitioner might agree with her, but Tris didn't want to leave anything to chance. Not with Cov, and not with their babies.

He swallowed.

Their babies.

He definitely needed medical reassurance that everything was okay. Her loss of weight worried him in spite of her reassurance that it wasn't a concern.

"How about you just give me this one? No arguments. After this we'll discuss everything to do with you and the babies and decide together, but right now I need you to see a doctor. And I'll be honest and admit it's not about you or them, it's about me."

Cov turned that smile on him, the one that made him feel a thousand feet tall and invincible, gutted and weak in the knees all at once. "Okay."

"Damn." He grinned. "You gave in too easy. That's going to bite me in the ass at some point for sure."

"Oh good, you're still here."

They turned to see Kirby walking toward them.

"I wrote down the details for you, Covington." Kirby held out a piece of paper. "I added my cell number too."

"Thanks." Cov took the note.

"What's this?" he asked.

"I invited Covington to Books and Bitches," Kirby explained.

"Books and Bitches?"

"Yep."

"Is this the book club Chief Murdock's wife goes to?" he asked, not really wanting the answer.

From what he'd heard around the station house, it was more like an excuse for the women of Winter Lake to get together, drink wine, and gossip.

Kirby grinned. "That would be the one."

"Oh." He frowned.

"Don't worry. We don't have any dirty little secrets about you to reveal. Although..." Kirby's gaze lowered to Cov's midsection. "I'm sure there's some we could discover."

Before he could argue for or against that proclamation, Kirby waltzed back down the hall and vanished.

"Don't worry. I won't tell them anything."

He returned his gaze to Cov. "I'm not worried about what you'll tell them."

"Then why is your forehead all scrunched up and your mouth threatening to split in half with the frown dragging the ends down off your face?"

"Because I've heard rumors about that book club."

"Oh, really? Anything juicy? I could use a little excitement in my life."

"I think you'll be getting plenty of that in the next few months; hell, with two babies it'll be years of excitement, so maybe you shouldn't go. Keep things calm and easy while you can."

"Why, Tristan Harding, are you scared of a group of women getting together and talking?"

He didn't like the grin on her face. He knew that grin. It meant he'd somehow challenged her and she'd do the opposite of what he'd suggested.

"Damn it." He sighed. "You're going, aren't you?"

"Yep." She nodded. "And you're going to take me."

Recoiling, he blurted, "I can't go to book club. It's a women's thing."

Cov laughed. The beautiful sound vibrated along his skin and into his bones, sinking deep until he felt it in every corner of his body.

He'd missed that laugh. The sweetness of it. Her pleasure so audible, so apparent.

"You need to do more of that," he said, stroking a finger over her cheek before gripping her elbow and steering her out of the hallway and back to their table where their dinner waited.

"What?" she asked.

"Be happy."

CHAPTER 9

"I don't need new boots," she argued.

"Yes. You do." Tris gripped her chin and locked eyes with her. "When the snow is thick on the ground, you'll want them. Your feet will freeze otherwise."

"But—"

"Cov, you need boots and a jacket."

"Fine. But I can pay for them myself." She tipped up her chin, daring him to disagree.

"Okay, you pay for the boots and jacket and I'll pay for the new pants and shirts you need."

"What?" she gasped. "You can't—"

"Are those my babies?" He pointed at her belly.

Covington eyed him through narrowed lids. "Oh, I see where this is going."

"Yep. I'm the reason your clothes don't fit, so I'm paying for ones that do."

"Tristan," she whined. Yep, she went there. In her defense, she was getting tired.

They'd been in Winter Lake Wears for half an hour, and in between arguing over who was paying, answering his questions about when she'd first realized she was pregnant and how she'd felt about it, she'd tried on outfit after outfit.

She had been surprised to discover the store had a large selection of maternity wear and there was now a pile of new clothes at the register waiting to be paid for.

They'd moved to the outerwear section, Tris insisting she needed boots and a coat. She'd concede on the boots, maybe, but she didn't need to spend hundreds of dollars on a jacket when she could just borrow one of his if she needed to.

"You need them, Cov." He palmed her cheeks, his hands warm against her skin. "I know you're probably worried about money. I won't get into it here, but we should talk about that. For now, let me do this. I *need* to do this."

She could see the truth in his gaze. She understood him enough to know he felt guilty for not being there for her before now and with a sigh, she gave in and muttered, "Okay."

He grinned. "There, that wasn't so hard, was it?"

"Don't push it."

Pulling her close, he dropped his mouth on hers for a quick kiss. It was the second time he'd done that since they'd left Della's.

Both times, a rush of need had flooded her veins and

made her tremble. Swallowing her reaction, she smiled at him.

There was so much in his eyes. So many things neither of them had spoken of yet.

Their friendship, their night together—being parents.

They probably would have stayed like that, caught in each other's gaze, indefinitely if they hadn't been interrupted.

"Can I get those in your size?" the salesgirl asked.

"Oh, yes." Heat flooded her face. "Do you have them in a six?"

"We do. I'll be right back."

Covington watched the teenager head away and noticed two women near the back of the store staring at her and Tris. When one of them smiled and moved toward them, she nudged Tris.

He turned, a big smile stretching his lips before he stepped forward and pulled the slender blonde into his arms.

She couldn't stop the frown, nor could she stop the shaft of jealousy that shot through her. They remained in the tight clinch far longer than Cov thought necessary. Their familiarity spoke of history—*intimacy*—and something inside her cracked.

She'd never thought about Tris being with someone.

He hadn't dated—that she knew off—in all the time she'd known him.

And not once in the months since she'd shoved him out of her apartment had she considered the possibility of him having a girlfriend.

The idea gutted her in a way finding her fiancé balls deep in a bulimic plastic Barbie hadn't.

She must have made a sound because Tris spun around, panic in his eyes.

"Cov." He gripped her elbows. "What's wrong? Do you need to sit down? You're as white as a ghost. Here."

He urged her toward the bench running down the middle of the shoe aisle and pushed her down, crouching in front of her.

"Breathe. Nice and slow," he ordered as he pushed her head between her knees.

She hadn't realized she was sucking air like an Olympic sprinter after the hundred meter final.

"That's it, slower. Deeper."

Why couldn't she breathe properly? Her heart pounded, her chest hurt, and her skin was coated in a slick layer of sweat.

"Here." A bottle of water was thrust between them. "I haven't opened it."

Tris took the bottle and twisted off the cap. Easing her up slowly, he held it to her lips. "Small sips, baby."

She tried. Except her breath still came in short and sharp. Stars danced in her vision and her whole body felt tingly, numb.

"Covington," Tris barked. "Look at me."

Blurred gaze darting to his, she attempted to focus on the color of his eyes, not the panic swirling in them.

She wasn't sure where the bottle went but his hands cradled her face now, his thumbs stroking her cheeks in mesmerizing sweeps that drew her attention. Leaning forward, he brought his forehead to hers.

"Breathe with me, Cov. Nice and deep and slow."

"Should I call the clinic?"

Cov glanced up only for Tristan to snap her gaze back to his.

"Eyes on me."

The pain in her chest eased, her breathing evened out, and the sound of her heart in her ears no longer drowned out everything around them.

"That's it. Keep going."

"Tristan?"

"What?" he growled, his eyes still glued to hers.

"Do you want me to call the clinic?"

He raised an eyebrow and Cov didn't need him to speak to know it was her call.

Shaking her head as much as his hands would allow, she croaked, "No. I just need a minute."

"Here. Try this now." He held the bottle of water to her lips and she sipped at the cool liquid, finding some relief from the burning in her chest. "Good?"

Nodding, she took another sip of the water and chanced a look at the women beside them.

The salesgirl had returned, her face scrunched in concern but it was the woman who'd given Tris the hug who looked the most concerned.

"I think you should go to the clinic. Just to be sure. In your condition, you can never be too careful."

Cov couldn't be sure, but she thought a flash of pain moved through the other woman's eyes.

"We're going there later. I'm okay, though, just a little tired." She tried to reassure everyone.

There was no way she was going to admit to having a panic attack.

She'd had one once before in her life so she knew exactly what had happened. It was why it happened that worried her.

"Thanks for the water, Addy." Tristan moved to the bench beside her. "What do I owe you?"

"Don't insult me, Tristan." Addy glared at him.

He held his hand up in surrender. "Okay. Okay."

"We haven't been introduced." Addy held out her hand. "I'm Addy and this is my sister, Willa."

"Oh." Taking the offered hand, she said, "I'm Covington."

"Oo... You're one of us," Willa said with a little clap of glee.

"One of you?" she asked, confused by the small elfin woman's excitement.

"Willa likes to collect people with unusual names. My full name is Adelia and she's Wilhelmina," Addy explained. "Of course, neither of us go by those anymore. Not since our grandmothers passed. Being named after the older generations can be a pain in the ass in this day and age."

"Better than being named after your mother's hometown," Cov said with a smile.

"Oh, really? Good thing she wasn't from Rutland or Pottersville or something equally bad." Willa laughed.

"Are you in town for long," Addy asked.

Covington glanced at Tristan but didn't get a chance to answer before he said, "She just moved here."

"You're staying?" Willa smiled; this time her clap of glee was accompanied by a little hop.

"Yes, I... Yes." She nodded. She should own her decision to move here and be near Tris. With Tris? She wasn't sure where that stood now he knew the babies were his.

"You should join us for our next book club meeting," Addy said.

"Is that the same book club Kirby invited her to?" Tris asked.

"Kirby's in town?" Addy asked "I didn't think she was coming home for a few weeks yet."

Tris shrugged. "No idea about that, but she and Race were at Della's a little while ago."

"Oh, come on." Willa tugged on her sister's arm. "We need to see if we can catch them before they head out."

"We do. It was lovely to meet you, Covington. Don't be a stranger. We own Booked." Addy waved her hand toward the front of the store. "It's the book shop down the block. Come by any time."

"See you later, Covington," Willa called over her shoulder as she headed for the door. "C'mon, Addy, let's hustle."

Shaking her head, Addy rolled her eyes and said, "Talk later," as she followed her sister from the store.

"I'm sorry." Tristan shrugged. "They can be a little overwhelming."

"Oh, I didn't have a panic attack because of them." Too

late she realized what she'd said and cringed waiting for Tristan's reply.

"A panic attack? I thought that's what it was. Want to tell me what triggered it, and since when do you suffer from them?"

Sighing, she tipped her head to the side and leaned on his arm. "Can we talk about it later? It's not a thing. I've only ever had one before."

She could feel him studying her and held her breath. She really didn't want to get into it here, and if she were honest, the afternoon had done her in and she really was tired, and they still had to finish up here, pay for her stuff, and get to the grocery store.

"You're wiped out. We should get home so you can rest."

"No. Let's finish this then get what we need at the grocery store. I'll be fine if we take it slow, and we have to be at the clinic later too." She couldn't stop the yawn her words brought on.

"We'll get done here then I'll take you home. I can come back out to get the food while you nap."

"If I nap now, I'll never sleep tonight."

"I really think—"

"Please, Tristan. I'm okay. Promise." She grabbed his hand and gave it a squeeze. "But I am tired enough to not argue when you try to pay for everything."

"Deal." Grinning he added, "And I have a witness to that, don't I, Jem?"

"You do. Let's try these on to be sure they're a good fit."

Between the salesgirl and Tristan, she was outfitted with new boots, gloves that fit properly, and a jacket in less than ten minutes.

Cov leaned into his side while he handed over his credit card and Jem bagged all her new clothes.

She knew she was relying on him a lot, more than she should, but right now she didn't have the energy to argue, never mind do for herself.

She'd be sure to make up for his support later. As soon as she got her feet under her again, she'd be better. More independent, not as much of a drain on his time or money.

She didn't like being beholden to anyone. It was why she'd never moved in with Gavin in spite of the numerous times he'd asked. And thank god she hadn't. What a disaster that would have been.

Stifling another yawn, she let Tris lead her out of the store.

CHAPTER 10

Tristan's words kept replaying in her head. Not that she needed them to. He'd spent the last few hours making sure she *was* happy.

Anything she wanted, he bought for her; anything she needed they couldn't find, he arranged to get. If he didn't stop, he'd have her spoiled rotten in less than a week.

"You okay? Do you need another pillow?"

Covington laughed. "I've got three now; what would I possibly do with a fourth?"

His gaze traveled from the top of her head to the tip of her toes. "Under your knees…?"

He had her stretched out on his couch, a pillow behind her head, one supporting her back, and the last one tucked under her feet.

She'd kept her mouth shut when he'd started 'making her comfortable' because she was tired after their dinner and shopping, and just the thought of arguing with him was too exhausting to consider.

"I'm fine," she said, covering a yawn with her hand.

Tris glanced at his watch. "We've got just over an hour before our appointment with Jared. You should sleep."

Sleep sounded good. Except there were bags and bags of groceries in the kitchen that needed to be put away and then there were the three bags of new winter clothes he'd insisted she needed that she had to wash...she stifled another yawn.

"Maybe a few minutes with my feet up."

The constant fatigue she'd thought a result of her lack of food consumption in the last few months hadn't improved since she began eating anything and everything again. Something to ask the doctor about later...

Covington wasn't sure what time it was when she opened her eyes. The room was dark, the blinds closed, and someone—obviously Tris—had covered her with the softest blanket she'd ever snuggled under.

Grabbing the edges, she tucked her hands under her chin and wriggled deeper into her comfy cocoon.

"Oh, good, you're awake. We need to leave for the clinic in a few minutes."

"Really?" So much for resting for a few minutes. Rubbing the sleep from her eyes, she sat up. "I guess I crashed."

"You've done a lot of sleeping today." He frowned. "Are you feeling sick?"

"No. The nausea hasn't been as bad in the last few days."

Come to think of it, other than the anxiety over telling Tris about the babies churning her stomach, she hadn't felt sick at all.

She'd passed the twelve-week mark on Tuesday last week and since then she'd pretty much felt normal.

Well, except for the clumsiness. And the urge to eat anything she could get her hands on. And the need to pee every other minute. And the sudden bulge of her belly. And the...

Okay. Not so normal.

"Covington."

Her gaze snapped to Tristan's. "Huh?"

"Do you have to use the bathroom before we go?" he asked as though he'd been asking the question for hours.

Damn. She was doing that a lot too. Zoning out. Her mind would get on a track, and like a train, it seemed to have only one direction to go.

"Covington." He clicked his fingers in front of her face. "Where the hell do you keep going?"

"Sorry." She forced a smile to remove the worry from his handsome face. "Yes. I need to use the toilet before we leave."

He eyed her for a moment before offering her a hand.

Covington let him pull her to her feet. "I won't be long."

"Okay, I'll wait by the front door."

Halfway down the hall she remembered she needed to grab the file her doctor in LA had given her. He'd included his cell number in case she had any trouble before she managed to find someone to take over her care. Made her promise to look for a new doctor as soon as she was settled.

Which kind of played into Tristan's insistence on seeing Dr. Groves.

She grinned as she ducked into the bedroom in search of the bag she'd put the file in. Of course she'd looked through everything, including Tris's closet and under his bed, before she remembered it was in the big suitcase she'd left in the trunk of her car.

"What the hell are you doing?"

Turning fast, she straightened from her position on the floor beside the bed, lost her balance, and bumped her head on the bedside table when she fell on her butt. "Ouch."

"Jesus, Cov." Tris was next to her in a heartbeat. "Where did you connect?"

She didn't need to answer. His hands roamed all over her head, stopping only when he couldn't find any sign of damage.

"You don't have a lump but that's not always a good thing." He palmed her face and studied her eyes. "Can you see properly? Vision blurred? Doubled? Feel dizzy or sick?"

"Relax. I'm fine. It was just a little-bitty bump on the head, not a life-threatening injury." She pulled out of his grip and stood. "I need the suitcase that's in the trunk of my car."

"Oh."

"Actually, that reminds me. Where is my car?"

"Er..." He looked away.

"*Tristan.*" She narrowed her eyes. "What did you do?"

"Well…"

"Where. Is. My. Car?"

"At the mechanic."

"Why?"

"I asked Larry to take a look at it."

"Why?"

"Because it's a rust-bucket death-trap and probably should be put out of its misery but I figured you'd freak out if I sent it straight to the scrapyard."

"It is not a death-trap." She loved her Cavalier. She'd had it since the day she'd gotten her license. Used every penny of the money she'd saved working two part-time jobs to buy it. The car had served her well.

"I notice you didn't argue the rust-bucket description. And how can you say it's not a death-trap when it coughed and spluttered its way up the street when you got here. I don't know how it made it from one side of Winter Lake to the other, never mind from one side of the country to the other."

She huffed. Hadn't she thought more than once on her trip that the old convertible wouldn't make it? Dammit. She hated that he was right.

Signing, she said, "Fine. A mechanic should look at it."

Tris laughed. "Jeez, Cov, don't let my concern for your safety twist your arm."

Rolling her eyes, she poked out her tongue.

He moved before she blinked. Swooped in and planted his mouth over hers, sucking her tongue between his lips and dancing his across it.

The kiss was unexpected, the flash of sensation, the rush of emotion, not so much.

She remembered kissing him. Remembered that his lips on hers had a way of wiping her mind clear of everything but him. More. More of him.

Whimpering, she softened, her body leaning into his, her arms sliding around his waist in an attempt to find an anchor. To hold on to the one solid thing left in her world.

The kiss went on and on until they were both gasping for breath.

Pulling back, she stared up at him, her gaze searching his for an answer. To what question she hadn't a clue but if she looked long enough, deep enough, surely she'd find the clarity she was looking for.

"Cov."

Her name whispered through his lips. The ones wet from their kiss. And she remembered hearing that tremor in his voice too. Being in Tris's arms brought back so many memories.

Like a movie reel, they rolled across her mind delivered in Technicolor brilliance with the added bonus of remembered sensation, taste, and smell.

He'd played her body so effortlessly that night. Stroked her skin and marked her soul-deep with every brush of his flesh on hers. She hadn't known anything like it.

Tris had loved each and every inch of her with such desperate enthusiasm that she'd been helpless to do anything but surrender. Returning his passion with an urgent fervor of her own, she'd indulged in fantasies she'd never dreamed of fulfilling.

It was the most amazing night of her life.

And she'd thanked him by shoving him out the door the next morning and keeping their babies a secret for months.

Taking a step back, she pulled out of his arms. "I'm sorry."

"For what? I kissed you. I should be the one apologizing." He dragged a hand through his hair before rubbing it over the stubble on his chin. "I shouldn't have touched you. It won't happen again."

"I'm not sorry about the kiss." Was he insane? Who in their right mind would be sorry about a kiss like that? She might have what people referred to as 'baby-brain' but she was with it enough to know there was nothing to be sorry for in that kiss.

"What are you apologizing for then?" he asked.

She wanted to smile at the look of confusion on his face but didn't think it would help the situation. "I'm sorry I threw you out. Sorry for whatever horrible things I said. I didn't mean one word."

He tipped his head to the side and regarded her with shrewd eyes. "You don't remember what you said, do you?"

"Ah..." Covington shook her head.

"Jesus." A bark of laughter exploded from his chest. "Shit. You don't remember a word and didn't mean any of them anyway, and I tucked tail and ran because of them."

"Oh." He'd left because of what she'd said?

Shaking his head, he said, "Yeah. Fucked that up royally."

"I—"

He dragged her in, gave her a quick squeeze, then spun her in the direction of the bathroom. "Go. We're going to be late."

"But—" He gave her a slap on the ass. "Hey!"

"Get going. I'll call Larry about your bag. We'll swing past the garage on the way to the clinic."

"Tristan—"

"Cov, baby, one thing at a time. Right now you need to see a doctor for my peace of mind. And you promised you wouldn't argue about this. Plus Jared is staying late just to see you so there's that to get you moving too."

Dammit. Did he have to remind her this was about him more than her? She owed him so much. He was so generous in spite of her turning up out of the blue with a couple of buns in the oven that happened to be his.

She didn't understand why he went out of his way to take care of her. It wasn't only because of the babies either. He'd been caring and considerate—hell, he'd offered to marry her—before he'd known he was the father.

Except he hadn't brought up the subject of marriage again. Not since this morning. Wouldn't he push for that more now he knew the babies were his? Should she bring it up?

No. Not when she'd said no and meant it.

Her mother had married a man who didn't love her because she'd gotten pregnant and look where that had gotten *her*. A lifetime in a loveless marriage with a faithless husband.

The last thing Covington wanted for herself or her children was a house full of desperate unrequited love and silent loathing.

No. She might be a little in love with Tris but she knew what they were—friends who'd fallen into bed with each other one time. Nothing more than two bodies enjoying mutual pleasure. And now the tiny babies growing in her belly connected them on an intimate level for life.

Except what was with their chemistry? Was that a side effect of pregnancy hormones? How could she trust anything—lust or emotion—when her system was short circuiting every other second?

She knew how she felt about Tristan before, then they'd had their one night and things had gone haywire, and when she thought she might have a handle on those emotions she'd discovered she was pregnant and anything before didn't matter.

Everything was upside down and inside out and flipped over. The one thing she was certain about was she should never have said yes to Gavin's proposal. But if she hadn't, she never would have met Tristan, and as much as her life had turned into one big soap opera, she didn't regret being with him or having his babies.

She could only hope they remained friends once the dust settled. But you didn't kiss a friend the way she'd just kissed Tristan.

That had to stop. As much as she wasn't in control of her hormones, she had to keep her lips and hands off him.

For both their sakes, they needed to stay firmly in the friend zone.

CHAPTER 11

BEING careful to avoid the potholes in the dark carpark, Tristan guided Cov toward the clinic. They were a few steps away when the door swung open, the man they'd come to see smiling at them from inside.

"Come in."

"Hey, Jared, thanks for staying open late for us," Tristan said as he ushered Cov through the entry ahead of him. "I really appreciate it."

"No problem." Jared closed the door and turn to Cov. "And this must be my new patients."

"Yes, Covington Valenti. Thank you for seeing me on such short notice, Dr. Groves."

"Well, we can start with that official Dr. Groves thing, but I hope we get to Dr. J or Jared before we meet your little ones. Tristan mentioned you have a copy of your file from your previous doctor; do you mind if I go over that while you get settled in the exam room? Oh, and before we start, is Tristan allowed in during your appointments or not? It's completely up to you."

"Hey!" he protested as he handed over Cov's medical file. "They're my babies."

"Yes, I believe they are, but currently they're wrapped up in this lovely patient who definitely is not your baby."

Jared grinned to soften his words but it didn't help. Tristan did not like the idea of being kept out of the room while the other man examined Cov regardless of his doctor status.

"It's fine. Considering my condition, I don't think there's anything he hasn't seen before," Cov laughed.

"Not seen, no, but perhaps heard? Have you listened to the babies' heartbeats yet, Covington?" Jared asked as he led them deeper into the clinic. "I'd like to do that tonight and if possible get you back here tomorrow for an ultrasound so we can take a better look. Of course, that depends on what I read in your file."

"Whatever you think is best. I wasn't sure if you were able to take over my care or if I'd have to go to a bigger town for the rest of my pregnancy," Cov said as she entered the room Jared opened for them.

"Unless there are special needs that crop up during the pregnancy, we should be able to deal with everything here even with you expecting twins. You haven't had any issues so far?"

"Just some weight loss due to morning sickness that hung around at all hours." Cov grimaced and Tristan's stomach clenched. He hadn't been there for that. Hadn't supported her through those weeks. "Don't get that look. It wasn't your fault you weren't there."

"How do you know what I'm thinking?" he asked.

She shrugged. "Don't really. Lucky guess."

"Hmm…"

"Okay, I'll just go over this while you get comfy in one of those highly fashionable gowns we doctors make you put on." Jared grinned. "Be right back."

The door swished closed behind him leaving them alone and suddenly Tristan felt uncomfortable. "Are you sure you're okay with me being here? I can wait outside until Jared comes back," he offered.

"Really? Tris, don't be stupid. You've seen every inch of me, and while some of those inches have already stretched in different directions, I'm more than happy to have you with me." She swallowed, her eyelids lowering, her lashes hiding her eyes as she murmured, "I want you here."

Without thinking about it, he reached out and pulled her against him. "I'm here. Right where you want me, whenever you want me. I just need you to tell me to back off or come closer or whatever. I don't want to make this hard for you, Cov. But I really, *really*, want to be there for every step from now on. I missed the first few months. I won't miss any more unless it's what you want."

"I want to do this together. We made them together. I know we didn't mean to, but we did, and I get that I haven't given you a choice in this and it's a lot to drop on you this far in, but I wouldn't want to be doing this with anyone else."

"Me either." He dropped a kiss on her head then moved

her to arm's length. "Let's get you out of that coat so you can get into that flattering green gown."

Smiling, Cov let him remove her coat and boots before she started to undress herself. She was stripped down to her underwear in seconds, and he found it hard to breathe, the room far too warm.

He averted his eyes and swallowed hard while he held out the gown for her to slip into. When she turned her back to him he realized he'd expected her to step into it but of course Jared would need access to the babies so the gown needed to go on in reverse to what he was used to.

"You okay? If you don't want to stay, you don't have to," Cov murmured over her shoulder as she moved to the exam table.

"What? No. Sorry." He shook his head. Tried to shake loose the lust fogging his good sense. "I'm a little nervous. This is a first for me."

"Me too. I heard the racing thuds that the doctor said were two heartbeats once before but I was too shocked to take notice of what they were pointing out on the screen. It will be nice to do this together." She held out her hand and he grabbed it with both of his.

"I—"

"All right, you two. Everything looks great in your reports, Covington. We'll keep an eye on your weight gain for a while but I don't envision any further issues. You said the nausea has settled down in recent days which would tie in with you hitting the second trimester."

"Yes, the last week has been pretty much free of it and my appetite has returned. I've been eating anything I can get my hands on. I managed to keep up the prenatal vitamins in spite of the vomiting too."

"Good girl." Jared rubbed his hands together. "We'll start with basic things. Temp and blood pressure. We'll do your weight last. I'd like to have a feel around your tummy if you're okay with that. Just for my own reference. You file is detailed and I could probably forgo it, but I'd like to handle you the way I would any other pregnant patient coming through my door for the first time."

"Whatever you need to do and whatever Tristan needs to know." Cov grinned. "He's been out of the loop with this, so he's got some concerns you might need to address."

"Ah, already a concerned daddy. Got it." Jared winked at Cov. "Okay, Tristan, what do you want to know?"

"She's lost weight. A lot by my estimation and I'm worried about what that means for her and the babies."

"Understandable. It's not uncommon for women with morning sickness to lose weight in the first few weeks; some even do it before they know they're pregnant. I had a look at the scan dated two weeks ago, and both babies look on track for the due date so I'm going to assume we'll see Covington regain that weight and put on more in the coming weeks. The loss certainly hasn't affected the growth of the babies."

Every muscle in his body seemed to let out a sigh. He hadn't realized how worried he was about it until Jared said he shouldn't be.

"I told you it was okay."

He glanced at Cov. "I know, but you've been sleeping

and crying since you got here, and don't get me started on that mild panic attack—"

"Panic attack?" Jared's head snapped up from where he was feeling around Cov's stomach. "What panic attack?"

"I'm fine. It was earlier today. Everything just got overwhelming and I was tired and as Tris said"—she shot him a dirty look—"it was mild."

"Get them often?"

"No. That was only my second. The first was when they told me I was having twins."

Jared chuckled. "It's normally the dads who have the panic attack then."

Tristan appreciated the attempted at lightening the moment but he could all too easily see himself having a panic attack after being told his woman was having two babies. "You better give me a prescription now then. I see plenty of anxiety in my future."

"With two babies, my friend, you'll be seeing plenty of action good and bad, but I think you have what it takes to survive. You run into burning buildings for living, don't you? Parenthood is a similar experience."

"Oh? How many kids do you have?" Cov asked with an arched eyebrow.

Jared threw his hands up. "Sorry. Those words come from years of observation. I've yet to experience the joys of fatherhood myself."

"It can't be that bad," Cov mumbled.

"I'm told it's as good as it is bad, but not one parent has ever admitted to me they wished they'd never had kids, so that should tell you something."

"They're too panicked to know?" Cov asked with a laugh.

"Possibly. But I'll tell you what I've told all my first-time parents. I'd swap places with you any day of the week if I could." There was something that passed through Jared's eyes before he smiled and changed the direction of the conversation. "Okay. Time to get a listen to these two peanuts."

It took him a few moments to get the first heartbeat pulsing through the air but when he did, the hair all over Tristan's body stood on end. The rapid thump-thump-thump filled his ears and sank into his bones. That was his baby. His and Cov's. *Their baby*.

"Sounds good." Jared moved the device around Cov's stomach until he was almost leaning right over her. "Ah, there you are, you sneaky devil."

Thump-thump-thump.

"Also good. Strong, the right speed." Removing the device from Cov's belly, he sat back on his stool. "All right. I'm happy to put off the scan for another week or so but with the storm rolling in over the weekend if you can swing by tomorrow I'd like to get it done then. Other than that, and let me be clear, I'm completely happy with the progress you've made so far, I'm only requesting the early scan so we can get comfortable with this new arrangement. It's not ideal to change doctors partway through and I want you both to be assured that I'm on top of any possible issues."

"We can come in tomorrow." Cov eyed him. "Can't we?" he asked with a sheepish smile.

"Yes. That's fine. Can we get a picture? I didn't last time. I didn't even think to ask."

"I can give you a copy from your file now. But yes, we'll make sure you have pictures to take home tomorrow."

"Okay. Thanks." Cov grinned.

"What time should we be here?" Tris asked.

"Whenever, we'll squeeze you in around the rest of the patients." Jared patted Cov's knee. "Hop up and we'll get your weight then you're free to go home. I'm going to prescribe rest as your blood pressure is a little elevated to what you've presented with so far, but I think that might be because of exhaustion due to the last few days of travel which, as your doctor, I will advise against doing again."

"Oh, it's high? One of the handouts they gave me in LA said high blood pressure could be a problem with multiple births." Cov scrambled to sit up and Tris lunged forward to help her.

"Should she be on bed rest?" he asked.

"No. But don't go driving across the country or running a marathon."

"Ha! No chance of either of those. I'm done with driving for days on end, and let's be real, I might be a professional dancer but running is not one of my exercises of choice."

"A dancer? Not sure you'll be able—"

Cov held up a hand to stop Jared's words. "Don't worry. My balance went at the same time as my ability to eat. I won't be dancing until after these two are born."

Jared frowned. "You lost your balance?"

"Yeah," Cov answered as Tris helped her off the table.

"I'm not sure if it was to do with the nausea or just pregnancy in general, but I'm a complete klutz now. I'm bumping into things, and if I move too quickly, I'm dizzy."

"We'll see how that goes. I don't think it's anything to worry about but I'd like to make sure there isn't anything underlying going on."

"My other doctor didn't think so."

"I tend to agree but I'll make a note of it anyway."

"Oh, hey, all that junk food was good for something." Cov beamed. "I've put on four pounds."

"Since you left LA?" Jared asked.

"Well, no, since two weeks ago when I had my last appointment."

"We'll take that number as an improvement but every scale is different so we can't be sure that's the exact amount you've gained. We can say you are gaining and that's our goal so we're happy."

"Do you always have to put a disclaimer on everything?" Cov asked as she stepped off the scales. "It's kind of depressing to think of it that way so I'm going to ignore you and go with my answer."

Tris laughed. "No point arguing with her on that."

"Those sound like the words of experience."

"They are."

"Oh, and what experience would that be, Tristan?"

Cov folded her arms across her chest which didn't have the desired effect, he was sure. The gown opening had parted at some point and she was currently flashing him and Jared half a boob and everything below her belly button.

The direction of his gaze must have given her a clue because she glanced down and gasped. Spinning around, she put her back to them. "Can I get dressed now?" she grumbled.

"Yes. I'll meet you both out front." Jared's laughter wasn't quite hidden, but the man made it out of the room before he laughed outright.

Tris moved closer to Cov and wrapped his arms around her waist, putting his chin on her shoulder. "I only meant, once you make up your mind you stick to it."

"Sometimes I shouldn't."

He stiffened. "Meaning?"

"I knew things weren't right with Gavin. Knew I wouldn't—*couldn't*—marry him and yet I never broke it off."

"I'm not sure that's the same thing as what I mean, Cov, and staying true to your word isn't a bad thing."

"How?" She glanced sideways at him. "How is staying engaged to a man I didn't love a good thing?"

He didn't know how to answer her. Couldn't find the words to tell her she wasn't in the wrong for keeping the promise she made when she took Gavin's ring. And that killed him. Because if she wasn't wrong, did that mean she was wrong to break it?

Had she loved Gavin in spite of his asshole behavior?

Did finding him with another woman destroy that love or did she still feel it?

Tristan wasn't sure he wanted to know the answer to that but he wasn't sure they could move forward if he didn't.

CHAPTER 12

HE CROSSED his arms and said for the millionth time today, "You're not going."

Covington blew out a breath. "Yes, I am."

"No. You're. Not."

Slamming her hands on her hips, Cov argued, "For god's sake, Tristan, it's just a group of women getting together and talking. We're not climbing a mountain."

"The doctor ordered you to rest."

She rolled her eyes at him. "I have been resting and I'm not running over to Lindsey's. You're going to drive me. The most active I'll be is a couple of trips to the bathroom, which is all I've done for days."

"One day," he argued. It had only been one day—not even twenty-four hours—since they'd seen Jared. But it felt like a billion of them with the amount of complaining Cov had been doing.

He could hear the frustration in her voice, see it on her

face, and knew he'd have to give in on this.

Except the thought of her out of his sight for a few hours gave him hives.

How the hell was he going to cope when he went back on shift in the morning?

Forty-eight hours without seeing her would kill him.

He didn't want to think about the things she'd get up to without him here to remind her to rest. Or think about the huge storm heading their way. The forecast called for eight inches in one day. The one day he wouldn't be home.

"Look. I know you're worried. I am too, but Dr. Groves said my blood pressure was only a little elevated from my last check up and could be attributed to the long drive and lack of sleep," she reasoned.

He knew all that. Knew he shouldn't be as worried as he was, but that didn't stop him from coming up with numerous worst-case scenarios. Which was why he'd bought a blood pressure machine.

Although he hadn't told her about it. Hadn't shown her everything that had arrived with the UPS guy this morning. Not after she'd freaked out when he opened the box of pregnancy books.

So he'd bought a few. Ten was a few, right?

"Please. If I don't get out of this house soon, I'm going to go postal and beat my head against a wall." She threw her hands in the air then gripped her head and crossed her eyes for emphasis.

Tris cocked one eyebrow. "Dramatic much?"

"Ha! You're not the one who's not allowed to lift more

than a glass of water or walk more than five steps without being yelled at."

He grinned. "Yelled at?"

She let go of her head with a sigh. "Okay, fine, not yelled at exactly."

Reaching out, he drew her close and tipped her face up to his. God, he wanted to kiss that mouth. He hadn't touched her in a sexual way since yesterday.

In spite of the fact they had shared his bed last night, he'd managed to keep his hands—and lips and let's not mention any other body parts—to himself. But she had this pout thing going on and she looked so cute in her frustration that he couldn't resist dropping his mouth on hers for a brief kiss.

"All right. I'll drive you to Lindsey's." Her grin blinded him. "But you're only staying for two hours, not a minute more, and I'm checking your blood pressure before we leave and again when I pick you up."

"Okay. Whatever you say." Her smile dropped, her eyes narrowing "Wait. How are you going to check my blood pressure?"

"I bought a machine."

"You bought..." She shook her head. "When? You haven't left me alone for five minutes. There's no way you could have gone to the shops without me knowing."

She looked at him as though she'd cut his knees off if he admitted to sneaking out without her.

Laughing, he planted another kiss on her lips before tucking her in closer and holding her tight. "I bought it online."

"When?"

"Same time I bought all those books you turned your nose up at. Last night. After you went to sleep."

He'd watched her for hours, the glow from his phone screen the only light in the room, while he'd Googled all manner of things to do with babies and pregnancy.

Eye opening were the words he'd use to describe his late night activities.

His brain was now filled with far more information about a woman's body and what happened to it during pregnancy than one man could handle. But it was his heart that was overflowing.

In the dull light of his bedroom, with Cov snuggled up next to him sound asleep, he'd had an epiphany.

He was completely in love with her.

Totally, irrevocably in love with Covington Valenti.

The mother of his children.

And he had no idea how she felt about him.

He knew she at least liked him. They were friends—close friends—long before they'd made love. Made babies. But that didn't mean she loved him.

She'd been engaged to another man. Willing to pledge her heart and life to someone else only hours before she'd let Tris kiss her that first time.

She wiggled against him and his cock perked up with interest. That particular part of his anatomy had been making itself know more and more over the last two days. How he'd kept from jumping her was anyone's guess and a fucking miracle.

When she wiggled again, he couldn't hold back a groan.

She stilled instantly. "Sorry. But…"

"What?" he ground out through clenched teeth. He wouldn't push himself on her but suddenly he was perched precariously on a tightrope of restraint.

"I have to pee," she whispered into his chest.

He laughed. Of course she did. It was the one truly predictable thing about her.

"It's not funny." He couldn't see it but he heard the pout in her voice.

"You'd think it was if you knew what had been running through my mind while you did your little need-to-go dance."

Her hips bucked forward, the swell of her belly pressing against his length. "I'm pretty sure I can guess what you were thinking."

"Cov." He couldn't keep the apology out of his voice.

She pulled from his arms and met his gaze. "It's fine. It's not like I haven't thought about it."

With that parting shot, she disappeared down the hall. A moment later the bathroom door closed and he stood there, mouth agape, mind spinning.

Had she just implied she'd been thinking about having sex with him?

They'd cuddled, kissed. He'd held her hand and cupped her belly to feel the shape, connect with the babies, but he hadn't done any of that in a sexual way. Yes, their contact was intimate, the most intimate of his life, but it hadn't been erotic or held any intent.

Not that he hadn't thought about having her naked and under him.

Their sexual attraction—well, his at least—was the pink elephant in the room. He saw it but ignored it. There was no way he could do that now.

He hadn't wanted to push her, especially after Jared said her blood pressure was up. He still thought they should get married. More so now he knew the babies were his.

He'd kept quiet though, concentrating on making sure Cov saw a doctor, got plenty of rest, ate the right food. It was the only way to stop himself from dragging her down to the court house and putting a ring on her finger and a signed certificate in her hand.

But now she'd pointed out the elephant...

It felt as though she'd thrown flammable liquid on his libido. In a flash it had gone from smoldering to inferno and he didn't stand a chance in hell of putting this fire out. Not without a cold shower.

Or sixty.

Or maybe just a bucket of ice to rest his balls in.

"C'mon, we should get to the clinic before we make Dr. Groves stay after hours again."

Tris glanced at the time. She was right. They were going to be late if they didn't leave now.

He'd called this morning to see what time would be the least busy and Georgia, Jared's nurse, told him to come in near closing time as the last few appointments weren't booked.

And while he'd been on the phone to the clinic, Cov had been on the phone with Kirby. That was why they'd spent the day arguing over Books and Bitches.

It seemed his ordered-to-rest woman had been putting an escape plan in place.

He'd even received a text from Lindsey assuring him they'd take care of Cov, make sure she didn't do anything strenuous or blood pressure raising. Then Addy had called to check on Cov and remind him of the book-club invite.

They were ganging up on him, he knew it. He liked that the women of Winter Lake were welcoming Cov into their fold. And really, he was overreacting. Her pressure had been fine when he'd sneakily taken it while she took a nap not an hour ago.

Sighing, he moved toward her. "Fine. I'll drop you off at Lindsey's after the clinic *if* your blood pressure is within normal ranges."

And while he wasn't happy about being away from her, maybe it would give him time to get his libido under control.

"You already agreed to me going; you can't put strings on it now," she said as she shoved her feet into her new boots.

"I said I'd check your pressure so it's an existing string, I'm just reminding you of the conditions of you going." He reached for their coats, smiling at the sight of them together on the coatrack.

"How about we let Dr. Groves decide?"

He could see this going against him but nodded. "If he says it's okay, then I won't say another word against it."

Jackets on, he opened the door and quickly got the house locked up and Cov into the warmth of his truck. Cranking the heat, he reversed out of the driveway and headed for the center of town. The clinic was close enough to walk, but in this weather and with Cov being pregnant that wasn't happening.

Pulling up into the spot closest to the clinic door, Tris was out of the truck and round to Cov's side before she'd managed to undo her seatbelt. He'd admit some of the rush was the excitement he'd been trying to keep at bay since Jared had said he want to do a scan today.

He wouldn't be the first dad to anticipate seeing his unborn child. Cov had the changes in her body as proof but other than the ones visible to the outside world, he only had her word that their babies were inside her.

Not that he doubted her at all; it wasn't that. And it wasn't that he needed to see to believe; it was more that he *wanted* to see them. Wanted to put his own eyes on them and make that connection.

The emotional connection was already there. It surprised him a little how quickly that had formed. Especially when he'd been completely blindsided by Cov's pregnancy. Shit. He'd even thought someone else was responsible for knocking her up.

"You okay?" Cov stared at him from the passenger seat.

He smiled. "Yeah. I'm just a little nervous. This is the big moment."

"The big moment." She cocked a brow. "I'm pretty sure the big moment was four months ago."

"Ha ha." He helped her out of the truck and closed the door. "It's the moment we meet them for the first time."

Opening the clinic door, he let Cov go in first. Georgia

greeted them and took them straight back to the exam room they'd used the day before.

"I'll just let Jared know you're here and then we can get started. You can either pop a gown on or just lower your pants enough for us to get at your tummy. My advice it to go with the gown. That way you won't end up with gel on your clothes," Georgia said before slipping from the room.

In a few moments he'd get to see his children. His future. He already felt connected to them. It was different from the way he felt about Cov. He wanted her by his side, wanted to be a family with her and the babies they'd made, but the babies...

They brought out an emotion he'd never experienced before. It was an extension of himself somehow, entwined with the deepest part of him and he hadn't even laid eyes on them yet.

"Are you ready?"

Tris turned to find Cov already stretched out on the table, gown on. "How? What?"

Laughing, she reached out a hand. "You were lost in thought. Care to share?"

"Huh." He shook his head. "No. It wasn't important." He couldn't tell her what he was thinking when he couldn't really work it out. Maybe once they saw the babies he'd be able to explain it.

"Let's do this," Jared said as he came through the door. "Before we start, are we wanting to know the sex if possible or are we keeping that as a surprise?"

"Can you tell this early?" Cov asked.

"Sometimes. I just want to be sure I don't spoil the surprise if that's what we're going for."

Tris looked at Cov and shrugged. "I don't think I care either way so whatever you want to do."

"I don't want to know." The words rushed out of her mouth. "I mean I do but not yet. Can we find out later?" she asked Jared.

"Sure. For now I won't mention anything I might see." He smiled. "Now let's take a look. The gel will be cold at first but will warm up quickly. Tristan, if you head around the other side of the bed, you'll have a better view of the screen when I'm ready to show you."

Doing as told, he made his way to Cov's other side and grabbed her hand. He watched the scanner move over Cov's belly, listened to the clicks of the keyboard as Jared measured and photographed. As the seconds ticked by, sweat broke out on his brow, slicked his back.

Finally he'd had enough of the torture. "Is there a problem?" he asked, the panicked edge clear in his voice.

"Not a thing, just takes a little longer when there are two bodies to measure and check. Ready to see?" Jared asked, his gaze still glued to the screen they couldn't see, his fingers clicking away at buttons.

"Yes," they chorused.

CHAPTER 13

"AND THAT RIGHT there is arm number four."

She blinked. Stared at the black and white image on the screen and wondered how Dr. Groves could tell what anything was.

He was pointing out another arm and she still hadn't worked out the last one. Or the one before that. Or that. It was all some weird deep space looking image to her.

Tristan on the other hand seemed to know before the doctor could point things out.

"Even when you tell me what I'm looking at, I can't see it," she murmured.

"It takes some getting used to. The pictures should help," Jared offered.

Tris waved a fistful of snapshots with a wide grin.

She was helpless to do anything but return his smile. He'd been so quiet when Dr. Groves had first turned the screen toward them. Covington was pretty sure he hadn't drawn a breath for a full minute.

The tears that filled his eyes had her own stinging, her throat tightening, and she was just a little proud of herself for not bursting into tears.

It helped that the images on the screen—pictures of what was happening inside her—had her struck dumb.

They were moving. Arms. Legs. Fingers. Toes. Heads. Everything seemed to be in perpetual motion and she couldn't feel any of it. Not even a flutter. She'd been struggling to grasp the concept of two little humans growing inside her and now...

Now she wasn't sure she'd ever fully comprehend the miracle that was occurring inside her body. And if she believed Dr. Groves, and let's be real, the man was a doctor —he knew what he was talking about, *she* was making those two miracles happen without doing anything.

Vomiting, crying, and falling over not included of course.

Every goal she'd ever had and reached paled into insignificance beside what she and Tristan had managed to create.

"Hey." Tristan leaned over, his eyes on hers, and hand cupping her jaw. "You okay?"

The tears she thought she'd escaped burst out. It was as if someone pulled a plug and let them free. Within a second she was a stammering, blubbering, dripping, snotty mess, pressed against Tristan's chest, soaking his sweater.

"Shh... it's okay. Everything's fine. Jared said the babies are healthy and growing at the rate they should be."

"I know," she sobbed.

His hand cupped the back of her head, pressed her face right over his heart, and she knew he didn't understand what had her crying buckets. Again.

He just held her tight, cradling her against him with one hand, running soothing strokes down her back with the other.

She had no idea how long it took for the tears to dry up but when she finally managed to get herself together enough to lift her head, they were alone. The equipment turned off, the lights on low.

"Where did—"

"He was already finished taking measurements and checking the babies so he took the reports to his office."

"Oh."

"You okay now? Want to talk about what that was?" Tris asked with a skeptical lift of his eyebrows. "Or not."

"Hormones?"

Chuckling, he tucked her face against his chest once more. "I see a pattern here."

"It's all so overwhelming."

"Well, I'll be honest, I'll take a crying jag over a panic attack any day of the week."

"Don't joke about it. It's not funny. I'm a mess and I can't seem to control it or even understand why it happens."

"I think we just witnessed why it's happening, Cov." He pressed his lips to the top of her head. "You're incubating two perfect little people inside you, and if you weren't feeling overwhelmed I'd be worried."

"I'm worried it's a permanent state."

"What is?"

"Being overwhelmed." She tried not to rub her face on Tris's sweater but she needed something to clean up soon or she wouldn't be able to help herself. "We're having two babies. One baby is scary enough. Two..." She shivered.

"It'll be fine. *You'll* be fine. *We'll* be fine. We've got each other, and the second I tell my mother, you can bet we'll find her on our doorstep."

Oh God. She hadn't even thought about telling their parents. Her father wouldn't care. Her mother she wasn't so sure about, but Tristan's mother was the sweetest most genuine person Covington had ever met, and she hated the thought of disappointing the woman.

"She'll hate me," she muttered. What woman wouldn't hate the one who trapped her son with an unplanned pregnancy?

Tris laughed. "She most definitely will not. She likes you better than me."

"How can that be possible? I've met her three times."

A sigh lifted his chest beneath her ear. "She asks about you every time we talk. She's been very upset with me these last few months because I've had no new Covington news to impart."

"Better no updates than the one she's about to receive." She pushed out of Tristan's arms. "Do you see any tissues?"

He handed her a box he grabbed from somewhere behind her. "Here. And please, don't worry about what my mom will say or think. You're the only woman I've ever introduced her to where she not only remembers your name but asks about you regularly."

Cov mopped up her tears and blew her nose. She hoped Tris was right. Her own parents hadn't been neglectful exactly but they certainly weren't affectionate. In fact she couldn't recall a single time either of them had told her they loved her.

Mary Harding was the complete opposite.

The first time she'd met Tristan's mother, she'd been with Gavin and while Mary had welcomed Cov into her house with a warm hug, she'd barely said hello to Gavin.

Cov had never questioned Tris or Gavin about it; maybe she should have, or at least taken notice of the way a woman who appeared so generous and welcoming would dislike someone so obviously.

"You should probably call her and tell her," she said, yanking another tissue from the box. "It's not like we need to wait any longer to be safe like everyone suggests."

"We'll call her next week. After you're all settled and I'm on more than a forty-eight hour break." He tipped her chin up and examined her face. "Do you want to head home to clean up before I drop you at Lindsey's?"

"I'm still going?"

"You don't want to?"

"Yes. Yes, I want to, I just thought...never mind." She waved a hand between them. I'll use the bathroom here and wash my face. No need to head home." She pushed Tris back and slipped off the table.

She'd change and freshen up, then go spend some time away from Tristan and the thought of disappointing his mother. Funny how her own mother's opinion didn't faze her but Mary's did.

Cov had spent years under the disinterested eye of her parents and given up any hope of gaining their approval long before she became an adult.

Between her parents and Tristan's mother, it was Mary who she wanted her children to know, who *she* wanted to know. She could only hope that this unplanned pregnancy didn't destroy their existing relationship.

FOR THE SECOND TIME IN AS MANY HOURS, COVINGTON watched Tris walk away. Oh, he wasn't *walking away* walking away, but he was leaving her at Lindsey's. Again.

He'd delivered her to the book club gathering an hour ago satisfied she was in good hands and her blood pressure at an acceptable level. Not even a little bit high. Even after her emotional meltdown in the doctor's office.

The second reading—only minutes ago—showed it even lower in the normal range so he couldn't argue the night out was too much excitement for her.

She'd nearly died when he'd waltzed into Lindsey's house five minutes ago. He'd scanned the room and as soon as his gaze locked on her, headed in her direction.

Tris had always been alpha and Covington wasn't going to deny getting a little thrill out of it but having it directed at her? Holy hell. It was a wonder her blood pressure hadn't gone through the roof.

It was certainly spiking now while she watched his

jeans-covered butt strut out of the room. She sighed. Suddenly wishing her pressure had been up so he'd insist on taking her home with him.

Kirby's laughter drew her gaze.

"What? What did I miss? What's funny?" she asked, bringing her attention back to the women in the room.

"You two are," Kirby managed between chuckles.

Terra put her hand on Covington's arm. "What she's trying to say is you and Tristan are too cute. Sneaking looks at each other while the other isn't watching. It's kinda painful to watch actually."

"He looks at me?"

"Oh yes, he looks at you. Like he's a starving man and you're an all-you-can-eat buffet," Willa added.

"He doesn't. Does he?"

She knew he'd been interested in her earlier—she'd felt the physical evidence pressed against her stomach—and she couldn't deny they had chemistry. They'd proven that the night they spent together. But did his attraction come from the fact she carried his babies or because he wanted *her*? And did it go deeper than a physical attraction?

Covington frowned when Kirby laughed again. "I'm not sure this is funny," she muttered.

"No. It's hilarious. You two are so wound-up in the madness of your unexpected pregnancy, you can't see you're in love with each other."

"He doesn't love me. He's just being the upstanding guy he is and taking responsibility for his future children." It was the babies that had his attention. Her by default.

"Didn't you tell us he asked you to marry him before he knew the babies were his?" Kirby prodded.

"Yes, but he—"

"I'm pretty sure that goes well beyond *upstanding guy*," Addy pointed out.

"I..." Covington stumbled over Addy's words as they ricocheted through her head.

Did it go beyond Tris's honorable good-guy character?

He'd always helped her. When Gavin hadn't been around, Tristan had. In fact, now that she thought about it, Tris had been around far more than Gavin in the last year of their engagement. She'd even called Tris a few times when she couldn't get hold of her fiancé.

And he'd come running, every time.

Lindsey patted her arm. "You don't see how he loves you because you're too busy hiding how you feel about him."

"Oh, I don't..." Her heart did a funny squeezy beat thing. *Oh god*. Did she?

Had she been so involved in the drama of her life, she hadn't taken notice of her own feelings?

She'd be lying if she said she wasn't attracted to Tristan, but lust was only chemistry and a relationship couldn't be based on that alone. Gavin had taught her that. And while she'd had more in common with Tristan than her ex-fiancé, she'd never looked closely at their friendship—at how deep it went.

Now that someone else pointed it out...

"I need a drink."

"You've got one," Lindsey said, waving her hand at the virgin daiquiri she'd made just for Covington.

"I need a *real* drink," she clarified. "Something strong enough to give me the courage to talk to Tris."

Kirby smiled. "You don't need liquid courage for that."

"You're right." She swallowed. "I already feel like I'm going to throw up."

"You'll be fine." Lindsey patted her arm again. "Trust me. No man looks at a woman the way Tristan looked at you just now and rejects her."

"From what Josh has told me, Tris has been torturing himself over something since he arrived in Winter Lake. The guys at the station all had money on it being a woman. Seems they were right." Jess frowned. "They actually did put money on it too."

"Yeah, I, um, may or may not have made fifty dollars when you rolled into town," Dana said with a sheepish grin.

Covington stared at Tristan's fellow firefighter. "You bet money on Tris being twisted up over a woman?"

"Nope." Dana grinned. "I bet he'd fall like a house of cards at the feet of the first woman to come looking for him."

"But...how...what...?"

Dana laughed. "Don't get all worked up. It was obvious the guy was head over heels in love—"

"He's not. He can't be. He left!"

Dana arched one eyebrow.

"Okay, so maybe he had a reason, but still." Covington sighed. She had no idea what *still* was. "I can't believe how fucked up this whole thing is. I was engaged to his friend the morning these babies were conceived. What does that say about me? About him?"

"Considering you're here, I'd say it says you're in love with him," Lindsey said.

"I'm pregnant with twins and he's the father; in love or not, where else would I be?"

And that was the million-dollar question.

If she hadn't gotten pregnant, would she have come looking for Tristan?

CHAPTER 14

TRIS DIDN'T WANT to leave.

He wanted to call in sick.

Call around and see if someone else could cover his shift.

But he wouldn't.

She'd promised him she wouldn't leave the house. The snow was already coming down and it was supposed to continue into tomorrow and Monday with the biggest dump happening tomorrow afternoon.

He'd checked everything. The windows and doors were secure. The furnace working perfectly. She had a small room heater he'd purchased yesterday just in case. Cupboards and fridge were full.

No more stalling. He had to go or he'd be late for shift change.

Bending over he planted a kiss on Cov's temple.

"Hmm..."

"Shh, go back to sleep. I'm leaving for work. I'll call you later."

"Okay," she murmured sleepily before snuggling down under the bedding.

God, he really didn't want to go. More than anything he wanted to crawl back under the covers with her. Wanted to stay wrapped up in the quilt, their legs tangled together, holding her close.

They had so much to talk about. They should have talked yesterday but by some mutually—telepathically—agreed upon decision they'd spent the day hanging out instead. Like they used to back in LA. Well, except for his 'yelling' for her to take it easy as the doctor ordered.

After their second trip to the clinic and the mind-blowing sight of their babies inside her, she'd spent a couple of hours with the women at Books and Bitches and when he'd brought her home, he could see how much the time out had done to improve her mood.

The numerous naps she'd taken during the day had probably helped too. Since that first slightly elevated reading her blood pressure had remained within range, which had eased his mind.

Last night he'd picked up some food from Della's before picking her up at Lindsey's. The news of Cov's arrival had spread along the grapevine and everyone, even residents he hadn't met yet, stopped by to congratulate him.

A few had even asked when the wedding was, but he'd deflected those questions and gotten out of Della's the second he could.

They'd returned home and eaten a late dinner together curled up on the couch. Over dinner they'd talked more about the town and the people, especially the women she'd met at Lindsey's.

He'd promised her a trip to The Lodge for dinner later next week and a tour of the whole area if weather permitted. By the time they'd eaten their fill and cleaned up, Covington was dragging her feet and barely keeping her eyes open.

By nine-thirty Cov had been lights out, snuggled up to his side.

Tristan had carried her to bed, stripped down to his boxers, and crawled in beside her. The last thing he remembered before his alarm catapulted him out of sleep was holding Cov in his arms, her warm breath fanning over his chest.

If he thought walking away from her all those months ago was hard, it had nothing on leaving her now. Maybe it was because she'd gladly welcome him back into bed this time.

Or maybe it was because he finally knew what was at stake.

He might have to leave her to go to work but he'd never willingly turn his back on her again.

"Go to work. You'll be late. I'll be fine. Stop staring."

Tris chuckled. "Sorry."

"No, you're not." Eyes still closed, she smiled. "Go."

He bent over and kissed her. On the mouth this time. "I'll call you later."

"Bye."

Another quick peck and he turned away and forced himself to leave.

He'd organized a lift so Cov would have his truck in case of an emergency, but he had extracted her agreement that she wouldn't leave the house unless she absolutely had to.

Even then he'd made her promise to call him first. If he could organize whatever she felt the need to go out for without her actually going out, he would.

In spite of his tardiness, when he closed the front door behind him, Devlin sat in his truck next door, waiting. Jogging over, he opened the passenger door and jumped in.

"Hey," he said, and got a grunt in reply.

He laughed as Dev put the truck in reverse and hit the accelerator.

"Shut up," his friend mumbled with no real venom.

"Rough night?"

"Not everyone has a hot chick in their bed."

"Hey."

"What? You denying Covington is hot?" Dev asked.

"No. But she's not some *chick*."

"Nope. According to the rumor mill, she's carrying your chicks."

"Seriously? What the hell did you have for breakfast? Whatever it was, it's disagreeing with you," Tris said, his words laced with the anger suddenly burning through his veins.

"Take it easy. I'm only telling you what's flying around. It made it all the way to my mother in Florida. Damn woman was on the phone at five this morning asking why the hell I hadn't found myself a lovely girl to settle down with like that nice young man Tristan has." Dev shook his head. "I swear, all she talks about lately is how old she is and if I don't get moving, she'll be dead by the time I make her a grandmother."

Tris swallowed. "Sorry."

"Nothing to be sorry about. I was only stirring you up. Plus it's not like this is the first time my mother has gotten on my case about finding a lovely girl to settle down with."

They were quiet for a few seconds, but as the station house came into view, Devlin broke the silence.

"So are we happy or—"

"Happy." Tris turned to face his friend as they pulled into a parking spot. "I'd be even happier if she'd marry me."

"You've asked?"

"Yes. No. Sort of."

Devlin sat in stunned silence for a moment then burst out laughing. By the time he'd caught his breath, Tris was out of the truck and halfway to the door. Glancing over as Dev moved beside him, he wondered if he could escape the third degree he was sure was coming.

"Okay. So I'm a little confused. Did you or didn't you ask her to marry you?"

No escape. "I suggested we get married before I found out the babies were mine. We haven't talked about it since."

Devlin stopped. "You offered marriage thinking she was carrying someone else's kids?"

Tris shrugged.

"Jesus. You're in love with her."

"Of course I am."

"She's the reason you came here. You were running." Dev narrowed his eyes, clenched his fists at his sides, and took a half step forward. "You didn't take off when she told you she was pregnant, did you?"

"Really? You're asking me that?"

"Right, right. I forgot who I was talking to. You're that guy who's mooned over another man's woman...*oh shit*. It's her. It's Covington." Dev slapped his forehead. "Why didn't I put the pieces together sooner? Fuck. Does Gavin know?"

"I have no idea. Haven't spoken to him in weeks and Cov hasn't said."

"You need to clear that up."

"That's the least of what I need to clear up. He's out of the picture and has been since the day I—"

"Are you two girls planning to work today or spend it gossiping in the driveway?" Chief Murdock yelled from the front door.

"Shit. I need coffee." Devlin bumped shoulders as he passed. "C'mon, my shout."

"Really?" Tris asked as he followed.

"Hell, no. It's the rookie's job to fetch the coffee, right, Chief?"

Chief Josh Murdock smiled. "Normally I'd say yes, but I have it on good authority you're about to come into some money."

Tris groaned. He knew what the chief was talking about. His workmates might have thought they were being stealthy, but he'd known about the betting pool the first day it had opened. And Cov had confirmed it after Dana had revealed details at book club last night.

He didn't like that he'd been the subject of conjecture, but it was nothing less than he expected. Although he was used to being in on the betting, not the subject of it.

"Don't worry, Harding. They've started a new pool."

"Don't tell me." He held up a hand. "I don't want to know."

"Oh, I think you'll want in on this one."

Tris eyed his boss's smug grin. "Okay. Fine. What is it?"

"Isn't it obvious?"

Tris shook his head.

"They're betting on how long it'll take you to get your woman in front of a preacher."

Tris groaned. "Even I can't predict that."

"Here's some advice." Chief clapped him on the back as he passed. "Don't be a dumbass and hide how you feel. When it comes to the woman you love, leave the macho bullshit at the door and tell her you love her. There's no weakness in letting her know you can't imagine living without her."

"And if she doesn't feel the same way?" Tris asked.

Chief smiled. "Tristan, the woman packed up her shit and drove across the country for you. Does that sound like someone who doesn't feel the same way?"

"She's pregnant with twins. Mine. She needs help."

"Yes, she does, but she could have gotten help without upending her life."

"But—"

"Harding!"

Tristan spun to find Dana glaring at him, hands on her hips. "She dropped everything and drove thousands of miles to find you."

"I know." And he did. He got that Cov had made a huge sacrifice by giving up her life in LA. "But that doesn't mean she loves me."

Dana rolled her eyes. "Fine. Be a dumbass. But don't blame me when you let the best thing in your life slip through your fingers."

"Son." Chief gripped his shoulder and squeezed. "Love, true love, is a wonderful thing. It's complicated and messy and most of the time hard work. But it should also be unconditional. If your love depends on hers or you can't trust her with how you feel, then maybe you don't love her like you think."

With another squeeze to the shoulder, the chief left Tristan standing there to ponder what he should do. He knew how he felt, knew he loved Cov, had loved her for months.

Could he tell her without needing to know how she felt? Did her feelings change his? Was he scared of a bruised ego?

It had taken a beating at her hands before. Was that why he kept holding back?

He'd held back for months because she was with someone else.

Could he stand back and let this opportunity pass him by?

What did he have to lose?

As things stood now, they were going to be parents

together. Whether they were together or not, they would have that bond for life.

Could he live the rest of his days with only that connection?

No!

He wanted Cov.

He wanted their children.

He wanted it all.

He wanted to be a family in every sense of the word.

Now he just had to work out how to make that happen.

CHAPTER 15

C OVINGTON WATCHED the snow coming down outside as
the day slowly awakened and wondered if it was safe to
venture out there yet. She'd never seen snow before
coming to Winter Lake, and the way the flakes fluttered to
the ground intrigued her.

Of course she'd promised Tris she wouldn't leave the
house until he returned, and so far she'd stuck to that.

She glanced at the clock. Only a few hours until he was
home.

She'd begun counting down from the minute he'd
kissed her goodbye Saturday morning. She thought their
early morning exchange had been a dream until he'd called
her midmorning.

They'd been texting and calling for the last two days,
and in two hours and fifteen minutes, give or take a few,
he'd be walking through the door.

She couldn't remember ever anticipating Gavin's arrival

this much. Not even in the early days of their relationship had she watched the clock or held her breath.

The last two days had given her a lot of time to think, to contemplate, to sort out what she wanted. For herself and the babies. For her and Tristan as a couple.

More than anything, she wanted to see if they could be a family. She thought he had feelings for her, she definitely had them for him, and the babies weren't in question. She loved her two little peanuts more than she'd ever thought possible. And she figured their daddy would love them just as much.

But did he love her too?

Could they go from friends to lovers and keep both relationships? Keep them growing, thriving?

Snuggling under the blanket, she watched the snow flutter past the window. It was brighter today than yesterday. And the weatherman said the storm had moved on and the snow would stop completely by early afternoon.

Hopefully, she could convince Tris to take her out before it quit falling. She wanted to turn her face up to the sky and feel the wet flakes on her cheeks. Taste it on her tongue.

It seemed like a childish desire but she didn't care. She planned to channel her inner child so she'd be prepared to give her babies the best childhood she could. Closing her eyes, she imagined the three—no, four—of them outside, building snowmen and making snow angels.

Her eyes stung. They'd be a family. One she'd only just come to accept she wanted with all her heart. It was what she'd been looking for when she'd said yes to Gavin. Except he hadn't been the right man to give it to her.

They never would have been happy, probably wouldn't have made it to their first anniversary if she'd managed to convince herself to walk down the aisle.

She found it all too easy to imagine walking toward Tris. If she were honest, she'd have to restrain herself from running down that imaginary aisle. He'd offered to marry her before he'd known the babies were his. She'd said no. Did she have the right to change her mind?

It was a woman's prerogative, right? Changing her mind.

Rolling over, she tried to picture how Tristan would look when she told him she'd thought about his proposal and yes, she'd marry him.

The sooner the better.

Smiling, her mind drifted from one scene to another, their wedding, in the snow draped gazebo she'd seen by the frozen lake when Tris had given her a quick tour of Winter Lake the other day.

The moment the doctor handed them their babies. Toddlers playing in the yard, their pudgy legs pumping hard as they chased butterflies in the summer.

It was all so easy to imagine, to dream about...

A loud bang startled her enough that she kicked the blanket off her legs, threw her arms out in defense. Her gaze shot to the clock.

Seven-twenty.

She must have fallen asleep.

Somebody thumped the front door several times.

It couldn't be Tris. He didn't finish until seven-thirty and he had a key.

So who the hell was banging on the door like the hounds of hell were on their heels?

Scrambling to her feet, Covington shuffled across the living room in her borrowed socks. "I'm coming. Hold your horses. I'm coming," she muttered.

Going to her toes, she peered through the peephole. Eyes widening, breath catching in her lungs, she sank back down on her heels.

"Open up, you bastard!" *Bang! Bang! Bang!* "I know you're in there, Tristan. Your truck's parked in the damn drive. Open the fucking door."

Gavin?

Gavin was banging on Tristan's door?

What the hell was he doing in Winter Lake?

Had he followed her?

Why would he follow her?

No, wait.

He was yelling for Tris, not her.

But what could he possibly want with Tris?

"Open the door, asshole. You think you could knock up my fiancée without me finding out?"

"Ex-fiancée." She hadn't meant to say the word out loud never mind yell it, but she couldn't help it. The fact Gavin felt he still had a claim on her pissed her off.

A heavy silence hung for a moment before Gavin said, "Covington?", his voice laced with confusion.

"Shit." This time she whispered. Not that it made a difference now.

"Open the door, Covington." The handle jiggled. "Let me in, Love Bunny."

Love Bunny? Really? *Love Bunny?* Was he nuts?

The last time she'd seen him, he was staggering drunk and she'd made it perfectly clear that anything between them was over and she'd moved on. Of course she hadn't revealed the identity of the man who'd gotten her pregnant, but she'd made sure Gavin knew she was ecstatically happy and wanted nothing more to do with him.

Except he was here. On Tristan's doorstep calling her *Love Bunny* in that whiny way he thought was cute.

And she had no idea what to do. She thought she'd put Gavin and that time of her life in the past.

She was so damn tired of the drama.

So tired.

The urge to hide, to bury herself beneath the blanket on the couch and cry had her sniffling, her eyes and nose stinging.

Why had her life turned into a soap opera?

CHAPTER 16

Tris spotted the strange car in his driveway at the same time Devlin did.

"Expecting company?" his friend asked.

"No." He shook his head and focused on the house. His gaze zeroed in on the man standing at his front door, fist raised against the wood. "Shit. Gavin."

"What? Where?" Dev's gaze bounced from the road to the house and back again as he navigated the slick road. "I didn't see him."

"He's at the door."

"She let him in?" The truck slowed.

"No. I think he's knocking. He either just arrived or she's not opening the door." Tris unbuckled his seatbelt, ready to jump out the second Devlin stopped. "Shit. Stop the truck. Stop the truck!"

He had no idea what Gavin was doing here, but seeing

him pick up a potted plant and throw it against the door didn't bode well.

Dev pulled up behind what had to be Gavin's rental. "Go," his friend urged. "I'll call the cops."

Tristan's heart beat triple time as he sprinted through the snow. The path wasn't shoveled so it was slow going but he made it to the porch just as Gavin lifted another pot. Tris lunged. Wrapped his arms around Gavin's middle and crash-tackled him against the door.

Except they didn't hit the door.

Instead they sailed right through the now unobstructed doorway and crashed to the floor inside the house. The ceramic pot shattered on the timber flooring and Covington screamed.

It was that blood-curdling sound that sent his heart into cardiac arrest. For a split second, Gavin got the better of him and landed a punch to his jaw.

The pain that shot through Tris's head was enough to snap him out of his frozen state. With a speed and a thought process he'd never be able to recall, he got his ex-friend into a headlock and pinned him facedown.

In the next few minutes, the place exploded with activity. He had no clue where everyone had come from but suddenly his house was full of people in uniform he should know but couldn't seem to focus on—police and firemen and para-medics. It was the last, tending to a bleeding Covington that had him letting Gavin go and racing to her side.

"Cov, baby." Tris tried to pull her to him but someone pushed him back.

"Give us a minute. I'm pretty sure it's superficial but I need to clean her up a bit to be certain."

He swallowed the lump in his throat. Discovered another—bigger—one in its place. His chest ached. His vision turned a hazy red. Covington's face blurred in front of him.

"Hey. Buddy. You all right?"

The gruff voice sounded miles away. And there was so much red. It was blood. Cov's blood. She was bleeding and he could barely suck in a breath.

"Hold it together, Harding." Chief Murdock clapped him on the shoulder.

He wobbled, his knees threatening to give out except he was already on them. Kneeling beside a bleeding Covington while someone else tended to her wounds and the police removed a shouting Gavin from his house.

"What happened?" he managed to choke out through his closed throat.

"A flying shard of pot." Tris was pretty sure it was Matt Hogan who answered. "Clean slice. Not deep. But it's a head wound. They bleed the most."

"I love you."

"What?" three people asked.

The only one he was interested in was Cov.

He shuffled forward and was grateful when Matt finished applying the bandage and moved out of his way.

Tristan took Cov's hands in his and locked his gaze on hers. Taking a deep breath, he spoke from the heart.

"I love you. I have from the minute Gavin introduced

us. It wasn't right, it wasn't fair, but I respected you and him in spite of what I knew. I should have told you—"

"Why didn't you?"

"I..." he sighed. "I didn't want to hurt you. Couldn't hurt you. And I knew it would."

"But don't you see that by not telling me, by being my friend and not revealing what you knew, you hurt me more?" Her eyes were full of tears.

"I'm sorry. I've got no excuse except I'm obviously a coward."

"I wouldn't call you that." Her mouth tipped up on one side. "Your job is to run into burning buildings after all."

"No fire has ever made me feel fear like the one that just crippled me. God, Cov. The blood. Gavin. The blood." He closed his eyes and took a deep breath.

Her fingers squeezed his.

Opening his eyes, he leaned closer. "I love you. With everything I am. Give me the chance to prove it to you."

"Okay."

"I promise if you say yes, you won't regret it. I'll spend every day making sure you're happy. Making sure you and our babies have everything you need and want."

She smiled. Nodded.

"You'll never want for anything. Not... Wait. *Okay?*"

"Yes. Okay."

"You'll give us a chance?" he had to double-check he heard her right.

"Yes."

"Really?" He had to be sure.

"For god's sake, Harding, the woman said yes. Ask her already."

He glanced over his shoulder and saw they had an audience. A house full of police and firemen and was that Harry Windburn in the back there?

The Mayor of Winter Lake was in his house?

Shaking his head, he turned back to Covington. "Ignore them."

"I was."

"Oh, right. Well. About that chance. Does it include maybe, if it's what you want, of course, I mean it's not like we need to rush, although with the babies coming—"

"Jesus. Get to the point, buddy," Devlin groused.

Cov grinned at him. "Yes."

"What?" Tris wasn't following. The punch Gavin landed must have knocked a few screws loose because he could swear Cov just said yes and he hadn't asked her anything yet.

"Yes. The chance includes marriage. On one condition."

"What? Anything. Name it." He'd hand over his first-born. Oh wait...

"I want to go outside and feel the snow on my face while it's still falling."

"Outside? Now?"

"And I want to make snow angels and build a snowman."

"Ah, okay..." Tris glanced at Matt only a few feet away and raised an eyebrow.

"Sure. No sutures, barely a scratch really, so there's no

worries about a concussion or further bleeding now that it's stopped."

"Right." They were going to make snow angels and snowmen. Pushing to his feet, he held out a hand. "Let's go play in the snow."

She moved into his arms, hers sliding up around his neck, her face tipped up to his. "Oh, and Tristan."

"Yeah."

She smiled. "I love you too."

He grinned. He was pretty sure it was the goofiest grin in history, but he couldn't help it. She'd said she loved him.

Oh, he didn't believe it would be all sunshine and rainbows but Covington Valenti loved him and was willing to give him a chance.

It was all he needed.

She pushed to her toes and pressed her lips against his. "And I don't know what I did for you to love me like you do, but I'm glad I did it."

EPILOGUE

Months ago Tris had thought having Cov's love was the only thing he needed to make him happy.

He was wrong.

Dead wrong.

Right now he needed the damn doctor to do something.

His wife was in pain and no amount of back rubs or chipped ice or drugs seem to make it go away.

"One more should do," Jared said from his position between Cov's legs.

Yeah, Tris wasn't sure how he felt about the other man getting such a close-up view of his wife.

"I can't," Cov wailed.

"You can, baby. You're so brave and strong and you'll rock being a mom," he tried to placate.

"Don't you talk to me about brave and strong. You're

not the one pushing two fifty-billion pound bowling balls through your vagina!"

"Ah..." Tris closed his mouth and let her squeeze the shit out of his hand.

"Easy there, momma." Georgia stroked a hand over Cov's taut belly. "Here comes another contraction."

With an agonized cry, Cov bore down. Sweat rolled down her face and coated her chest. Her eyes were scrunched tight, her nose crinkled, and her hair lay plastered to her skin.

Tris thought she'd never looked more beautiful. He'd never loved her more.

"All right, here we go..."

Tristan's gaze snapped to Jared's face. The guy didn't seem panicked. Not like Tris was.

They were four weeks ahead of schedule, but everything had been textbook perfect up until now. They just needed to make it through—

A tiny wail of protest broke the air and tears instantly flooded his eyes, blurring his vision.

He leaned over, tried to see more of their first baby coming into the world. He saw a dark head...a wrinkly face...a pair of shoulders...and a perfect body with two arms, two legs, and...a penis.

Shit. He had a son.

"It's a boy, Cov. God. It's a boy."

"That's right, Dad, baby number one is a boy. And judging by the weight of this guy..." Jared held their son in his hands. "He's a good-sized one."

"Can I see? I need to see." Cov tried to sit.

"Hang on." Jared passed the baby to Georgia who placed him on Cov's bare chest.

Tris watched his wife stroke a fingertip down the little guy's check and didn't bother to hold back the tears.

They'd done that. Together.

Made that perfect little boy.

Cov gasped, her face contorting with pain.

"Okay, looks like this second one is in a rush."

Georgia scooped his son up in a blanket and handed him to Tris. "Step back, Dad."

He didn't go far. Wouldn't dare. And as he held his newborn son, he watched as the tiny form of their second child entered the world.

There was no cry this time and the smiles from before were replaced with frowns that had him taking a step forward.

"Tristan?" Covington's weak voice drew him to her. "What's happening?"

"I'm not—"

A wail only rivaled by the siren at the station house cut him off.

"And baby number two is a girl," Jared announced as he lifted up the tiny wailing baby, her arms and legs wiggling wildly.

"Jesus, she's got a set of lungs on her." He smiled. He'd take those screams over that dead-silence any day of the week.

"Yes, she does. How about we give Mom both babies and see what happens," Jared suggested.

"They're okay?" Cov asked, worry creasing her weary face.

"More than," Jared confirmed.

"But they're so early," Tris argued.

"Doesn't mean there will be problems. I'm not seeing anything that causes me concern. We'll take them one at a time in a minute to weigh them and check a few things, but what we have here is two perfect little bundles of joy."

Tris was pretty sure the bundle of joy screaming her head off wasn't so joyful. He moved closer to his daughter, his son still cradled in his arms.

"Hey, baby girl," he murmured near her ear.

Instantly the child hushed and turned her head towards him.

"She knows your voice," Cov whispered.

Both babies turned towards her. "And they both know yours."

With Georgia's help, they placed both babies into Cov's arms and Tris couldn't resist pulling out his phone and snapping the first shot of the three most important people in his world.

"Do we have names for these two?" Georgia asked.

He glanced at Cov. They'd discussed it and couldn't agree so they'd decided they'd get to pick one each, but now they had to work out who named who.

"You do the girl's one," Cov said with a smile.

"Okay." He nodded. He'd had a few girls' names he'd really liked but now that his daughter was here, he wanted to take her in a little longer before he decided. "Give me a minute to look at her."

"I think this guy looks like a Kane. Kane Tristan Harding."

"Cov." Tris could barely get her name out.

She smiled up at him. "I didn't think you'd go for Tristan as a first name."

"No. But I love Kane. And Tristan for a second name works."

"So what are we calling his sister?" she asked.

"Carys Hope Harding."

"Well." Cov lowered her gaze to their quietly resting babies. "I think Kane and Carys are going to give their parents a run for their money."

He swallowed the lump in his throat. He imagined they would.

And he wouldn't have it any other way.

If you enjoyed this book, please consider leaving a review. It only takes a few minutes and you'll be helping other readers find stories they'll enjoy, as well as supporting authors you love.

For what's coming next, latest releases, sales and more, join
Rhian's Royal Readers
http://www.rhiancahill.com/contact/newsletter/

ACKNOWLEDGMENTS

I have to thank Melanie and Shawna of Melanie Shawn for writing about a small town I was thrilled to 'play' in for a while.

When Kindle Worlds closed and I received the original version of Tris and Cov's story back I had no idea what I'd do with them. It was while I wrote a scene for a series I hadn't yet released that I decided I wanted to make them part of that world somehow. And so, Winter Lake was born, or at least expanded.

I can't wait to bring you the rest of these stories. And I'm really excited to bring you the Broken Bay series.

There's no way I can go without thanking my editor Fedora. She keeps me in line and doesn't yell at me when I run late and push us both to the very edge of deadline. I love you girl and I can't wait to work on the rest of this series and so many more to come with you cracking the whip and keeping me from jumping off the ledge (or making those horrible grammar errors I'm prone to make).

And where would I be without readers. Each and every one of you are why I keep writing, you're why I couldn't stay away from the words (and people in my head) even though I couldn't find the energy to deal with any of it. It's been a while but I finally found the joy in the struggle, because you, the reader, choose to spend time in a world I've created. Thank you. From the bottom of my heart, thank you!

xoxo

Rhian

ABOUT THE AUTHOR

Rhian Cahill is the alter ego of a former stay-at-home mother of four. With motherly duties rapidly dwindling, Rhian is able to make use of the fertile imagination she used to keep herself sane for all those years of slavery. Years spent living overseas and visiting tropical climates have helped inspire some steamy stories.

Multi-published in erotic romance, paranormal romance, and contemporary romance, Rhian, with the help of Mr. Muse, spends her days and nights writing.

When not glued to the keyboard you'll find her, book or knitting in hand, avoiding any and all housework as much as possible.

For more on Rhian –

Website – http://www.rhiancahill.com/
Newsletter signup – http://www.rhiancahill.com/contact/newsletter/
FaceBook – https://www.facebook.com/RhianCahillAuthor

Instagram – http://instagram.com/rhiancahill/
Twitter – https://twitter.com/RhianCahill
BookBub – https://www.bookbub.com/authors/rhian-cahill
Goodreads – https://www.goodreads.com/rhian_cahill

LOVE THE WAY YOU ARE
WINTER LAKE BOOK 2

Who needs 20/20 vision to find true love?

There's something familiar about the gorgeous woman across the crowded club. When he "accidentally" bumps into her, Alex Dean is shocked to discover what it is. The tall, leggy blonde is none other than Sadie Emerson, his college math tutor—and the subject of more fantasies than he could count. Years later, she's looking better than ever. He has to have her. Tonight.

Does it really matter that she thinks she's going home with his buddy, Alec Dane?

Apparently it does because she sneaks away the morning after. *Twice.* First, when she discovers her mistake, then when she decides her upcoming move to Winter Lake makes them a two-day stand at best. But the sex is off-the-

charts combustible, and Alex is already seeing stars,
hearing bells…envisioning houses and picket fences and
other things he'd never considered.

Now all he has to do is convince Sadie his feelings are real.
His shy wallflower might consider him a mistake—but
Alex has never been more certain.

Chapter 1

"C'MON. DON'T BE A CHICKEN." Mel took a sip of her margarita. "I thought this was the beginning of the new Sadie—"

"Dee," she corrected.

"What?"

"The new me is Dee not Sadie." A new name, a new woman. Or at least that was the plan.

Shame the name change hadn't boosted her confidence. It seemed she was still the same nerdy wallflower she'd always been—too shy to say hello to the hot guy across the room.

Mel waved her hand, her drink sloshing up the sides of her glass. "Sadie, Dee, whatever. Just go over there and say hi."

"You only want me to go so you can have a shot with one of the other guys."

"Well duh! Have you seen them?" Mel downed the rest

of her cocktail then fanned her face. "That's some seriously smokin'-hot man perfection over there."

Sadie sighed. Dammit. She couldn't even think of herself as Dee. So much for reinventing herself.

She glanced over Mel's shoulder at the group of men on the far side of the dimly lit club and murmured, "Comes with their profession I guess." Her eyes snagged on one man in particular. Tall, dark, and every woman's wet dream.

"What?" Mel leaned closer, hand cupping her ear. "You'll have to speak up, the music's loud in here."

Her friend wasn't wrong. Sadie's ears were ringing, and the thumping beat vibrated up through her feet and rattled her bones. She was pretty sure they could hear the music two counties over. "Never mind."

Mel reached for the pitcher and topped off her glass. Sadie quickly placed her hand over her own empty glass to stop Mel from getting her any more drunk than she was. Already she feared she was in for one hell of a hangover.

"I'm good."

"If you were, you'd go over there. You're not drunk enough if you're still sitting here with me." Mel attempted to kick her under the table—the six inch stiletto her friend wore barely skimmed Sadie's leg—and almost toppled off her chair.

Laughing, Sadie righted her. "Watch it."

Swaying a little, Mel gripped the edge of the table with both hands to steady herself. "Like you, I'm good."

Sadie arched an eyebrow. "Really?"

"No. Actually, I'm not. I need a strong, strapping hunk of man to take my drunk ass home, where he'll take complete advantage of my intoxicated state and deliver me to the stars."

"There's just one flaw in your plan."

"Yeah, I know." Mel sighed. Exaggerated a pout. "My best friend won't introduce me to the man in question."

Sadie laughed. "Besides that."

"Oh, you're just a ray of sunshine raining all over my parade tonight."

"You won't remember any of it come morning."

"With any luck I'll still be coming in the morning."

Sadie shook her head. After six years, she was still amazed by her friendship with Mel. They were opposites in every way. Mel was outgoing and the life of the party, while Sadie preferred to skip the party altogether. "Why are we friends again?"

"Because you need me to push you out of your shell. Force you to be social." Mel stood on wobbly legs and tried to drag Sadie out of her seat. "Now get over there so we can both get lucky."

"Fine." Sadie allowed herself to be pushed to her feet. "But I'm going to the bathroom first. These stupid contacts are killing me. I can't believe I let you talk me into getting them." The smoky air of the club had gotten in her eyes and dried them out. Not only did they hurt but she couldn't see clearly either.

"Excellent." Mel flopped back into her chair. "I'll wait here for my knight in shining armor."

Sadie watched Mel gulp the remainder of her margarita and top up her glass again. "You might want to slow down or you'll pass out before your knight arrives."

Her friend frowned at her drink. "Good point." She pushed the full glass across the table to Sadie. "You drink it."

She turned away but Mel grabbed her arm and spun her back.

"What have you got to lose? This time next week you'll be in Winter Lake, New York. At best you'll have a hot one-night-stand memory to take with you. At worst a bad one or none at all. Either way, you'll never have to see the guy again."

"But—"

Mel gave her arm a shake. "No. No buts. You can do this. You *need* to do this. Cut loose, Sadie. Be daring. For once, take life by the throat and give it a shake, go after what you want."

She was already doing that by walking away from the only life she'd ever known in the city to do what she'd always dreamed of doing. Live in a small town where she knew her neighbors and her life didn't make her head spin.

If she could find the courage to do that, she could manage a little more to take her across the room to say high to her college crush, right?

"You can do it," Mel encouraged.

Nodding, Sadie broke free of Mel's hold. "You're right. Dee Emerson, CFO of the Economic Development Board of Winter Lake, wouldn't blink at going over there." She *could* be Dee. She *needed* to be Dee. Her dream future depended on it.

"No, she wouldn't." Mel's lips curled in a smug smile. "Now drink that glass of courage."

Doing something she never did, Sadie picked up the margarita and drained it in one go.

She shuddered as the cold liquid slid down her throat, through her chest, and into her stomach, where it hit the pool of alcohol already in her belly.

Setting the empty glass down, she took a deep breath and turned to look at the group of men fifty feet away.

Her vision was blurred due to the new contacts irritating her eyes but she could still see—if a little fuzzily—Alec Dane and his group of friends with their usual entourage of women. She had tutored most of the guys in college—knew them by name; she shouldn't be afraid to go over there and say hello.

Sadie straightened her shoulders.

She *wouldn't* be afraid. Not tonight.

She'd go to the bathroom and remove the contacts then she'd wander past and pretend to notice them for the first time. Then she'd smile and talk like any other sexy, confident twenty-six-year-old, and maybe, just maybe, Sadie would get to live out her ultimate fantasy.

One night with Alec Dane.

Chapter 2

ALEX DEAN WATCHED THE BLONDE HE'D HAD HIS EYE ON all night weave her way through the crowd toward the bathrooms. Putting his beer down, he walked away from the redhead who'd been giving him the come-on for the better part of an hour without a backward glance.

He'd made it clear he wasn't interested except Red was either too drunk to register his brush-off or figured she could change his mind.

She might have had a chance if he hadn't already spotted the blonde.

Red wasn't the first to mistake him for his friend Alec Dane. Not only did they share a similar name, but they looked so alike they could pass for brothers, and during their rowdy college days, had on more than one occasion.

He kept his eye on the back of the blonde's head as he followed her through the crush of bodies. She was tall—taller than his usual type, anyway—so it wasn't hard to keep her in sight.

Something about her had struck a chord the second he'd laid eyes on her. He'd been staring at her for a good portion of the night and he still couldn't work out what it was that held him enthralled.

She disappeared into the women's restroom and he glanced around for a spot to wait. A small section of wall tucked around the corner from the club's main room formed an out-of-the-way alcove and the shadows meant he could watch her unseen when she finally emerged. Get a gauge of what it was—other than her being a knockout—that had his insides tight and his cock stretching to full length.

He settled in for the long haul—in his experience, women took forever in the bathroom—but it was only a couple of minutes before she stepped back into the hall.

She propped the door open for another woman to pass

through and the bright light from inside gave him a clear view of her face.

Alex pushed off the wall.

Sadie Emerson.

No wonder he'd been captivated. Alex hadn't seen her in three—no—four years.

She'd been the football team's math tutor his senior year of college and he'd had all sorts of fantasies woven around the studious sexy glasses wearing Sadie Emerson. And in his opinion, she'd only gotten hotter.

Before she could pass him, he moved into her path. "Hey."

"Oh." She pressed a hand to her chest. Took a half-step back. "Sorry. I didn't see you."

"My fault." He smiled down at her. Estimated she was around four inches short of his six-two.

"Alec?" She squinted, leaned closer and peered up at him. "Alec Dane?"

Alex's gut cramped. "Ah..."

"Wow. I haven't seen you in years. How have you been?"

He'd never objected to being mistaken for his friend before, but there was no ignoring the ball of acid currently burning a hole in his stomach. He couldn't say why he didn't correct her though.

"I'm good. How have you been?"

"Great. I'm great." She smiled.

They stared at each other for long seconds.

"Well. I, um, should get back," she said, indicating the noisy club behind him.

He stepped to the side and blocked her when she went to move around him. "Can I buy you a drink?"

"Oh." She licked her lips. Looked away. Glanced back. "Y-yes. Sure."

Alex put his hand on her lower back and steered her out of the hallway. Bending down, he brought his mouth close to her ear and pointed to the far end of the bar near the entrance to the club. Away from his friends—from hers. "Let's go over there."

Sadie nodded and headed in that direction.

The crowd thinned the farther away from the dance floor they went. He could have backed off, given her more room, but he liked the feel of her in front of him. The way his chest brushed her back, her ass against his groin every few steps. The scent of her hair as it floated around him— the heat of her so close.

Fantasies stored in the back of his mind came rushing forward. Lust-infused blood pounded in his veins and drummed in his ears, throbbed in his balls. His cock hardened, pressing against the fly of his jeans, the thick denim a rough caress over his bare shaft.

"This okay?" Sadie stopped at the end of the bar.

"Perfect." He leaned into the bar and angled his hips to hide his hard-on. Now they were here, Alex had no idea what to say to her. Glancing away, he tried to get the barman's attention.

"So...do you come here often?"

Alex turned back to Sadie. "No." He'd never been in this club before. It hadn't been around when he'd lived in the city for the four years he was in college.

"This is my first time." She looked around them. "Not sure it's really my thing."

"Oh? What made you come tonight?" He leaned closer so he could hear her over the music and her scent surrounded him. Filled him.

Her mouth kicked up in a half smile and Alex's gaze was drawn to her lips. They glistened under the bar lights but it wasn't gloss. She must have licked them recently. The thought almost made him miss her next words.

"My best friend. She can be pretty persuasive."

"Is that a good or bad thing?"

Sadie laughed, the sound a deep throaty rumble that came from true humor, not the fake kind Red had been dropping earlier. "Both?"

He couldn't tear his gaze from her mouth. Her lips were full, but not that bee-stung look a lot of women went for. Sadie's didn't appear medically enhanced at all and he wondered how soft they'd be, whether they'd open willingly if he pressed his tongue against the seam...

He gave himself a mental shake to clear the X-rated thoughts from his mind. "Ah, one of those friends."

She nodded. "Yep. But she means well."

"Most of them do." Alex noticed a barman working his way toward them. "What will you have?"

"A bottle of water."

Alex arched an eyebrow. "Water?"

"Yeah." She smiled. "I've had one too many margaritas already."

"You're drunk?" She didn't appear intoxicated to him, except he wasn't exactly an expert on Sadie Emerson.

"Let's say a little tipsy and leave it at that."

He moved closer and before he could engage his brain, lust was taking over and words were pouring out his mouth. "So I could take advantage of your *tipsy* state and steal a kiss?"

His eyes tracked the movement of her tongue as she licked her lips. Fire and need shot through his groin.

"No need to steal one," she murmured, looking up at him through lowered lashes, the action shy, not practiced.

It was all the invitation he needed. Alex didn't wait for her to say anything else. He reduced the distance between them and pressed his mouth to hers.

He flicked his tongue out and traced her lips before increasing the pressure along the seam like he'd imagined. She opened on a small gasp and he took advantage, thrusting deep to taste her heat, to stroke her tongue with his.

She moaned into his mouth, her arms going around his neck, and he wrapped his arms around her waist, pulled her fully against him.

Pressed together, mouths joined, the club—the music, the people—faded away, leaving nothing but the sweet taste of hot woman and urgent need. Her breasts were crushed between them, her nipples hardening by degrees as the kiss went deeper.

Alex couldn't stop himself from grinding his cock against her. His hips rocked forward and Sadie had to know what he wanted. Where this was leading.

He slid a hand up her spine and gripped the back of her

head, tangled his fingers in her hair. With the other, he palmed her ass, pressed her closer.

She melted into him.

A groan rumbled in his chest. They fit in a way that left him reeling. He'd never experienced such intense need from a kiss. He had to have more. More of *her*.

All of her.

Pulling back, he spoke against her lips. "Come home with me."

"Oh…" Her hot breath fanned over his mouth, her eyelids fluttering open to reveal her lust-dazed hazel eyes. "Y-yes."

Independent, career-minded Melinda Shaw has singlehandedly built one of Miami's premier event-management companies, but success hasn't stopped her heart from shifting its focus to marriage and children. Still, she's not about to burden a younger man with her fantasies of familial grandeur...until she does.

Their combustible sexual chemistry notwithstanding, Grady still has to work overtime to convince Mel he wants her despite their impending parenthood, not because of it. It'll take almost losing everything—and more than a few of Grady's famous moves—to score Mel's heart once and for all.

Wild Rush Of Love

Drinks aren't the only thing this barman is serving up.

Tending bar at Winter Lake Lodge, Rush Whelan enjoys all the fun with the female clientele, with none of the commitment. They come for vacation—and for Rush, in his bed—then they go. Until Sabreena. After spending her entire holiday together, Rush still can't get the shy beauty out of his mind. When he finds himself with some unexpected time off, there's only one thing to do—follow Reena home.

Waitress Sabreena Howe is grateful for the built-in family that comes with working at Pat's Pub. Mr. Collins and his brood have taken in more than a few strays, Reena among them. But even with their support, Reena has trouble letting people get close... including Rush. Despite their instant connection, Reena allowed fear to abort what could have been their amazing last night together.

When Rush shows up in Baltimore, Reena finally sets her trepidation aside, exploring her newfound sensuality even though she suspects another brief week together can only lead to heartbreak. Her home is here; Rush's is hundreds of miles away.

But the heart knows no time or distance. If Reena can redefine her definition of home, she'll find love is the greatest wild rush of all.

LOOK FOR THESE TITLES BY
RHIAN CAHILL

CONTEMPORARY ROMANCE

Everyday Heroes World

Flashback

Flyboy

Fallout

Winter Lake Series

Love Me Like You Do

Love The Way You Are

When You Love Someone

Let Me Love You

Wild Rush Of Love

Party Games Series

Truth Or Dare

Spin The Bottle

Pass The Parcel (novella)

Are You Game Series

7 Minutes In Heaven

Catch'n'Kiss

Red Light, Green Light

Hearts Are Wild Series

No More Talking (novella)

Dare You To (novella)

Mad Love

Boys Of Summer

Bondi Beach Boys

Sand, Surf And Sunnie

Only You Series

All Of You

Holiday Romances

Christmas Wishes

New Year's Kisses

Valentine's Dates

Secret Santa

Frosty's Snowmen Series

A Touch Of Frost

A Kiss From Kringle

A Taste For Kandy

Secret Confessions

Sydney Housewives – Virginia

Standalone Titles

Make You Burn

PARANORMAL ROMANCE

Coyote Hunger Series

Coyote Home

Coyote Wild

Coyote Whispers

Coyote Law (novella)

Coyote Lies

For a full list of available books visit

http://www.rhiancahill.com/books/

For what's coming next, latest releases, sales and more, join

Rhian's Royal Readers

http://www.rhiancahill.com/contact/newsletter/

www.ingramcontent.com/pod-product-compliance
Lightning Source LLC
Chambersburg PA
CBHW030801190726
48285CB00003B/970